ANOTHER MAN'S BED

ANOTHER MAN'S BED

T A Charnley

Published by New Generation Publishing in 2016

ISBN: 978-1-78507-843-9

www.newgeneration-publishing.com

Carol Davis knew that the violence was not over for tonight, even though she wished that it was.

Carol lay in bed, unable to sleep, wearing her white night-gown. She looked tired and haggard, and she was very still. Her face was discoloured by bruises around her mouth and face. Dried and crusted tear stains under her eye and marking her cheeks also contributed to the unhappy appearance.

Her hair though, strangely enough, in the bright light of the bedroom, appeared unharmed. After all she had been through, it had somehow managed to retain its glorious vitality. Her husband, Sean, had never really paid it much attention, so he'd never caused it much harm, but even her heavily-crushed spirit didn't affect her hair's appearance too much, even though it affected her own.

Sean was in the bathroom, getting ready to come to bed. Carol knew that he would be back any minute. She lay there, waiting for him. The bedroom light was on, but she didn't even want to look around. Her back would be towards him when he came in. The light glared at her. She would hear his hard, padding bare footsteps on the floor, coming closer as he came in from the bathroom.

She could hear him brushing his teeth and swilling out his mouth and spitting into the sink, then she heard the sound of him coughing. A rough, heavy sound. Strange how, at times, natural sounds like that were peculiarly comforting. They made him sound more human, even though most of the time, he didn't act like it.

A moment or so later, she heard the lavatory flush and the twing-twong sound of the bathroom light being turned off and the approaching threat of his returning footsteps. She tensed up even more.

Carol heard him come back into the bedroom and walk up to his side of the bed. His presence was strong, even though she couldn't see him, but she didn't need to see him. She knew he was there. It felt as if he was standing very close, right behind her in fact, when she knew he wasn't. It was one of those things.

She wondered now, if the violence would begin again, when all she really wanted was to get some sleep. It sounded strange, but it was at times like this when she couldn't help but regret marrying Sean, even though she knew why she had done so.

Their relationship had excited Carol from the moment they had met, nearly four years ago.

Carol had dated Sean for almost a year before they were married, having a steady relationship with him to begin with, but it rapidly moved on to becoming more intimate. She was only twenty-two at the time and possibly rather naive, but then, who wasn't at that age? There was a strong, natural energy and passion between them, even if, on the down side, it did often produce unpleasant tensions between them, something which both herself and Sean were obviously content to live with and accept. Every couple had their arguments. Why should they be any different?

Their relationship had always been strong however, even Carol knew that. Strengthened by an intensity that they both enjoyed – it was charismatic. Sometimes, it almost seemed to Carol that they were a combustible engine; often out of control, and loving every minute of its fast, thrilling and daring freedom.

Their personalities had been a strangely curious match. Carol had liked Sean's wild, exciting personality, and Sean had obviously seen something in her, a modest, innocent, but sexy appeal and charm. She was adventurous, out-going, and not afraid to try new things, and Sean had also liked her outside appeal, which gave Carol confidence.

She was a moderately slender woman, but not necessarily thin – more of a curvy, cuddly shape and she was very attractive, good-looking, fresh-faced, with a clear complexion, and lovely grey eyes – but by far her most distinguishing, dazzling, even pleasing feature, was her hair.

Carol had a head of wonderfully thick, and lustrous, neck-length auburn hair, gloriously full of body and bounce. Nearly every strand was wavy and shiny, like curled strands of silk. It looked like a fountain of copper against a blazing red sunset. It seemed to shine with its own natural energy, as if delighted in being alive. It was simply beautiful. Sean never mentioned it a great deal, but Carol was aware of it. They brought out something special in each other, something different, and of course, they enjoyed a good sex life.

There was tremendous excitement between them, a wonderfully satisfying lovemaking sexual chemistry. Sean may have been a little unpredictable at times, but that was simply part of the fun of their relationship together. He also made her feel protected. Carol had had every reason to believe in their future together, and so, in a rather short space of time some would say, they were engaged and married. Carol had no reason to believe she was doing anything wrong. She couldn't help but look forward to a very happy marriage, something she never would have dreamed of before she met him. There was nothing wrong with wanting that kind of pleasure out of life. Unfortunately, she would pay a heavy price for those expectations.

They'd been married only a month or so, when any hopes or dreams of that kind were shattered. Carol soon discovered a very different side to Sean, a side she didn't like, an unpleasant side, which made her realise the terrible reality of what she had got into. Sean's intense, powerful nature soon began to turn nasty and short-tempered, and he became violent.

It began with little things, although not so little at the time. Slapping her across the face when they got into arguments, sometimes so hard it would knock her back a few feet, especially when he felt himself losing or the argument got too heated. He would simply explode. Understandably stung and near tears, she would run off to the bedroom and hide. An apology would occasionally come afterwards, but the nice act wouldn't last long. There were other things too.

It wouldn't take much to make him turn on her. If she said or did something he didn't like, he would become cold and sarcastic, harsh in tone, verbally abusive and eventually, violent, slapping her again, even though she tried to ward him off, blocking him with her arms, pleading with him to stop and leave her alone, which often made him more angry. And sometimes, his frightening dark rages would mysteriously seize control of him for no reason at all, which terrified Carol; and it would begin again; the slapping around, shoving, shouting at her, verbal abuse, and there would be a horrific darkness in his eyes too, almost a savage glee, which made Carol wonder if he was secretly enjoying it and also how far he would go.

There were also his jealous rages too which Carol found just as terrifying. If not more so. Any attention from men – which she did get, mostly because of her amazing hair, but sometimes other things (like her bottom for example) – whether she responded or not, would also get an unpleasant rise out of Sean, who would take it as an insult towards him, and not as a compliment, which he would then take out on her at home. He would be intimidating, bullying, and his violence would be even more vicious; free swinging fists to her face and body, threats against her life, and eventually, as it had done several times – it would end in rape – brutally assaulting her much like an outside attacker – another intimidating weapon he would use against her. The way he did it made Carol shudder with revulsion.

Carol hated herself for being so vulnerable and naive. She felt hurt and angry. Although, most of the time, there wasn't much room for anger, only fear. Terrible, dark fear. Anger was pretty much a luxury.

She sometimes thought about escaping, running away to a shelter, but for some strange reason, it didn't seem like the right thing to do. She had no idea why. Surely she had suffered enough for her mistake. Surely she wouldn't have to suffer for it forever. Or maybe she would. Maybe a part of her felt she still belonged with him, regardless of all the pain. But wasn't it said sometimes that you had to feel the pain before you could appreciate the pleasure? Maybe so, but in this case, the pleasure had unfortunately come first, and now she only suffered the pain. And there really was no way out.

She had no intention of killing him either. No way. Absolutely not. She was no murderer. The consequences of that – going to prison, were even more frightening. She'd occasionally had dreams about that too. In fact, she'd almost been relieved to see him alive when she woke up.

On a few occasions however – one night in particular, while she lay in bed – Sean came close to killing her. The chilling memory of his voice, low and eerie, calling her name out and opening her eyes to see him standing there, leaning right over her and his hand then firmly coming down to cover her mouth, while his other hand tried to kill her was still painfully vivid. Even though it was more than a year ago, it still made her shudder. That unpleasant look had been in his eyes then.

Her back was towards him, but Carol could sense him standing there. She never knew if it was a good idea to look at him or not. It sounded as if he was fiddling around with something on his bedside table.

She wondered if he was standing there watching her, ready to do something. Maybe making her wait before he attacked her again. There was every chance it could happen. Carol felt her stomach quiver.

It had already been another rough night. The air was tight and heavy with the atmosphere of violence, both tonight and from other nights, when there were obviously other memories which she remembered, but tonight, ever since he'd come in from work at seven, a little later than he liked, and slammed the front door shut, reminding Carol again that she was trapped in this hateful, dark and terrifying life, the violence and abuse had been never ending. Sean's dark mood seemed in control of him tonight. Or maybe it was her.

During dinner in the kitchen earlier this evening, Sean oozed anger – perhaps a bad day at work, and breathed like a dragon as he ate, making Carol very nervous. She'd asked him if he was all right and he shouted back at her so viciously that it made her jump and she ended up near tears. Sean hated that.

'Don't you start that, you bitch, you shut up right now, I don't fuckin' need you,' he'd growled at her.

The pain was too much for Carol. Her hand covered her mouth, but she couldn't hide her tears or hold back the pathetic whimpering, and Sean's second warning to shut up only made it worse. So he lashed out. The next thing Carol knew, she was flying back off the chair, pain exploding through her face, hitting the cupboard behind her. She started crying, but she managed to get back up again and finish her dinner.

A little later, she was at the table drinking coffee, having a moment to herself while she had the chance, when Sean came out to get a drink. She got up to get out of his way, but he turned on her for no particular reason, possibly reminded of earlier and started slapping and punching her, even while she was down, as she had tried to defend herself after collapsing to the floor.

All that, and more, was the bruising, both on the side of her face, near to her eye, and the one beside her mouth. A jealous outburst a couple of days ago, which ended in another rape, also remained unpleasantly fresh. That had in fact been the last sex they'd had. These attacks were not as frequent at the moment, but they happened, that was enough. Nevertheless, it wasn't what had happened before that scared her, it was always the next round of abuse that Carol feared, the violence she *would* suffer, but never knew when. The violence that had gone before simply made her fear what was to come. It deadened the atmosphere.

There was an unsettlingly strong chance though, that it could happen again tonight. She sensed it more than anything. Perhaps that's why she felt so tense. Sean's dark mood of earlier had not subsided.

'Oi,' he said.

Carol seized up, wondering what he was going to do. 'Yes?'

Her back was still towards him, even though he was speaking to her. She was still afraid to look at him.

'I can't speak to you with your damned back turned, can I?' he said, coldly, his hard voice exploding through the air.

Carol's stomach suddenly twisted and tightened. That tone of his could have such an unnervingly steely edge to it. She looked around at Sean, who stood there on the other side of the bed, staring at her.

He was only wearing his pyjama trousers. His chest was covered in masses of dark blond hair. His mean but powerful dark eyes just stared at her.

'We may need some shopping tomorrow, I've run out of some stuff. You'd better go into town.'

'What about the off-licence?' Carol suggested, timidly.

'I ain't paying their bloody prices!' he snapped. 'Anyway, foreigners run it.'

'Okay, I'll go into town. Is there a list?'

Sean gave her a look which said 'What do you think I am, your assistant or something?'

'You'll have to make one out yourself,' he sneered, flatly.

Carol nodded, as if he had answered her nicely.

'Okay, I'll do it in the morning.'

Sean then simply looked away from her, acknowledging her in his own way, and turned on his bedside lamp before going back to turn off the light.

Carol still had a feeling the violence was not over for tonight. Then again, she nearly always had that feeling, but she honestly thought there was more to come. She remained very tense.

She couldn't help but glance quickly at his bedside table, wondering what he'd been fiddling around with earlier. His watch was there, next to his digital alarm clock. Nothing else. He'd probably been checking his alarm. He had another early start tomorrow, which he didn't like.

Sean worked for a building contractors. With his five-foot-eleven frame and medium-strong build, he was a natural at labouring work. He earned a lot. The trade paid well.

Carol suddenly looked away as he came back and sat on the edge of the bed. He got in next to her and the room went dark as he turned off the bedside lamp. Carol still felt as if the violence was not over.

The bed rocked and the mattress squeaked as Sean tried to get comfortable.

'Goodnight,' Carol said, wondering if that was it for tonight.

'Yeah, 'night,' Sean grunted back.

They were in bed for no more than a minute, when Carol suddenly had to go to the bathroom. The violence was not over.

She did not want to have to hold it in all night. There was a chance she could hold it in and risk wetting the bed, but she didn't know if it would spread to Sean's side or not, and that would make matters worse for the morning, with the smell of it all over him, maybe even *on* him and having to go to work like it.

And it would mean extra work for her, having to wash the sheets, and the mattress would probably need attending to as well. But the biggest worry was getting it all over Sean. It might not of course, but the odour of it could get on him, and he would say it had anyway. So, it was either laying there and holding it in and suffering until tomorrow and still risking getting punished by Sean because of the odour lingering to him, or relieving herself now and hoping Sean could hold his temper. She would be as nice and as quick about it as possible, not that that usually made any difference, but she knew she had to go.

Opening her mouth to tell him though, proved difficult. For a moment or so at least, the words just wouldn't come out. They were locked inside her, desperate for everything to remain calm and for things to stay as they were. But were there really any long-term benefits? The violence would start again before long anyway, but she so wanted not to disturb things now. Not to set Sean off again. But the need to speak up and just get it over and done with was still there. Maybe if she lay here thinking about it long enough, she would drift off to sleep, but that still left her original concern about getting it on him, messing things up for the morning.

Did she have a choice? Her heart hammered.

They'd been in bed for nearly a couple of minutes now and Carol's insides were starting to feel unpleasantly cold, as if someone was grinding ice-cubes inside her. Of course, she could just get up and go, without turning the lamp on, but that might annoy him even more. And that was just as difficult as speaking up. However, she must have been fidgeting a little because of it, for she'd disturbed him anyway.

'What are you doing?' he suddenly barked in the darkness.

She was almost thankful, but her heart hammered even harder.

'I'm sorry, Sean, I really am, but I have to go to the bathroom,' she said urgently. 'I won't be long, I promise.'

Carol was hoping that saying it nicely like that would diffuse it somewhat.

A terribly uncomfortable moment followed just seconds before his response. Sean made a sound like a growl and a snort in the darkness. She felt him roughly shifting next to her, and she thought he was going to do something to her right now, like grab her and hurl his fist into her face or something. She could hear his heavier, hostile breathing. She could also sense him sitting up in bed now looking at her. The thought of it made her shudder.

Suddenly, weak light filled the room again. He had turned on the lamp. Now she knew he was looking at her. She dared to turn around and face him, slowly. He didn't want to talk to her back. He was glaring at her.

'Why didn't you go before we got in bed?' he demanded, roughly.

'I'm sorry, it's only just come on,' Carol replied. 'I won't be long, I swear.'

His cold, dark glare cut right through her. 'You'd better move it,' Sean hissed.

Carol nodded. 'I will,' she said, and in a hurry, she threw back the quilt and practically ran to the bathroom while Sean lay there, propped up on his elbows, glaring hard into the semi-darkness, and snorting impatiently.

Carol would have liked to have gone quickly and come back, but of course, it took her a little longer than she wanted it to. Too long. Either way, it wouldn't have mattered.

Sean began to yell at her from the bedroom. 'Will you move it for Christ sake! I've gotta be up early tomorrow!'

It took her a good few minutes to finish, and by the time she was, Sean had already lost patience. And his temper. She heard his feet thundering onto the bedroom floor as he got out of bed. She flushed, quickly washed her hands, dried, and hurried back to the bedroom. Too late.

He stood there, hands-on-hips in the semi-lamp-lit darkness of the bedroom, glaring at her. Carol stood there, not wanting to go in. The room was cosily half-lit by the bedside-lamp, but with Sean's intimidating, hostile appearance and his furious countenance right there in front of her, it may as well have been total darkness.

He stared at her for what seemed like an eternity. The violence was not over.

'Get in here,' he growled.

Reluctantly, Carol stepped into the bedroom, and walked past him, still feeling his eyes boring into her.

'Sorry I took so long,' she couldn't help saying, as she walked passed him, even though she had only been a few minutes.

The click of the light switch and suddenly the bedroom light was on and its massive, harsh glare seemed to turn the bedroom into a huge, unfriendly void, filled with a terrible and dangerous presence.

Carol turned around, startled, to see Sean coming towards her. The furious pounding of his approaching footsteps was also enough to know what was coming next. Her mind only screamed, *No*! But what came out of her mouth was totally different.

'Sean, please, not ag—'

He struck her hard across the face, and she was thrown back with the force of it, bouncing off the end of the bed and hitting the floor with a painful thud. For a few seconds, the world spun, but she soon regained her senses and realised where she was. She was in a lot of pain. The hard slap had struck her in the mouth, cutting her lip. A speck of blood trickled out, which she touched with her little finger as she quickly tended to it. It stung. Fuzzy pain also exploded through the old bruises on her face.

She sensed Sean moving in again.

'Get up,' he growled down to her, breathing hard.

She just wanted to go to bed.

'Sean, please, no more,' she said, looking up through slightly dishevelled hair.

'I said, get up!'

He grabbed her, roughly, and pulled her to her feet. Another slap to her face followed, then another, from the left and right, and another, then another. Her mind screamed and wailed feeble, pointless protests, but her mouth emitted only tiny whimpering and squealing sounds, as each time he struck her, fuzzy, sharp and burning knives of pain exploded through her face. But that was nothing compared to what he did next. He made a fist and hit her twice in the face, and then in the stomach. Carol grunted hard in pain and fell to the floor, putting a hand to the side of her mouth, where the punch had hit her. Her face felt as if it was about to explode. The punch had also hit her where the old bruising was, and again, warm, sick, fuzzy pain buzzed fiercely through it.

She lay there holding her mouth and stomach, too tired to do anything, wanting to stay here on the floor where it seemed almost safe. The violence could have been over for tonight, but it was another one of those bad nights again. Although, on previous nights just like it, Carol had been hospitalised a few times for minor injuries that she had sustained through Sean's abuse, including one or two cracked ribs and deep bruising in various places. One particular night that stuck out was when Sean had been in an exceptionally vicious rage, really out of control, and, after causing her a bit of a bad fall, had also broken her arm, or so she thought. On that occasion, Carol had managed to get to the phone and call for an ambulance, which had come out in the middle of the night to take her to the hospital for treatment.

When it arrived, it had almost seemed larger than life with its flashing blue lights and white exterior, and it had been a welcome sight indeed, considering the fact that Carol didn't think it would even turn up. But of course, friendly sight though it was, it didn't change her situation.

The arm had turned out not to be broken after all, the swelling had been the result of a hard bashing. Of course, when she was there, at the hospital, being treated by a nurse, who had called a senior male nurse over, they had also discovered her other minor injuries. Maybe she simply came over as a battered wife, despite her pretty face and wonderful hair. Her face wasn't that marked up at the time. Injuries had been mostly on her body then.

She had not wanted to talk much about it when they were speaking to her. She wasn't sure what she had hated most; being there in the first place, or the looks of pity and, or disgust on their faces, and on those on some of the other staff.

The physical abuse was also the reason why they didn't yet have children. Sean wasn't even able to suppress his violence when Carol once became pregnant. Unbelievably or not, he hadn't even realised what he'd done until it was too late, it was almost as if he'd forgotten about her condition. As a result, she had suffered a miscarriage. Although, looking back, maybe it was a good job that they hadn't had any kids. Not much of an environment to bring them up in.

Carol looked up at Sean's monstrous shape as he glared down at her, too angry to bother about her bruised, cut and tear-stained face. She stayed as perfectly still as she could, not moving to defend herself, not even daring to look up at him for long. She was afraid of more violence, more pain. She just wanted this to stop.

'You've put me in a great mood now, haven't you!' he snarled down at her. 'I told you I've gotta be up early tomorrow! How can I get to sleep now?'

She sensed more to come.

He swung his foot back and kicked her in the stomach. Carol grunted hard in pain. Another kick to her stomach followed. And another. She felt even more defenceless and pathetic lying here taking this.

'Sometimes, you really make me sick,' he spat. Thankfully, he then stormed back to the bedroom door, kicking it shut, then he thumped off the light switch.

The cosy semi-darkness of the lamp filled the bedroom with nothing but unwelcome, ugly shadows, not in the least bit cosy at all. Carol watched, as Sean got back into bed, hoping he would soon calm down and hopefully fall asleep. The room went dark as he turned the lamp off again. She couldn't lie down here forever.

Carol eventually managed to get up and soon followed into bed, careful not to disturb Sean too much, and eventually she managed to get to sleep herself, even with the pain causing her extreme discomfort. They faced away from each other.

At least now, the violence was over for tonight. The time was nearly one o'clock. Of course, there was always the violence tomorrow to think about. But she could hopefully rest now. Stay in bed now and be still and make the most of the non-violent moments afterwards.

Sean would hopefully sleep for the rest of the night now and then in the morning he would go to work, so hopefully, she had some time before the violence could and would begin again. Even Sean had to rest sometimes. And heaven knows what mood he would be in tomorrow. The violence could be even worse. She didn't know. That was the terrible thing. That was her fear. But she could rest now and do the shopping tomorrow, like he said.

Sharp pain again burned in her face as she nervously licked her lip. The cut on it stung too. She lay there, still and silent, her eyes wide open to the darkness around her – and aware of Sean laying there behind her. Shadows played around in front of her, acting out the violent moments gone by. Her memory, vulnerable now, playing them back to her in cruelly vivid detail.

This was the cycle of violence. A never ending, dark and totally dispiriting experience, with no way out. But she would soon sleep. The violence was over for now. No more. Rest. Just rest and be still. No more violence now. But tomorrow. The fear was still inside her. Rest.

How was Carol supposed to know that tomorrow night, she would be spending the night in another man's bed?

★

Sean was at work. He'd gone off this morning without so much as a word. A temporary reprieve. Carol had tidied herself up as best she could. She'd showered, bathed her face and washed and brushed her hair. She'd also tried not to think about the day ahead, especially tonight. She was scared enough as it was.

Earlier on, she'd made a shopping list, had watched morning television for a little while with a warm cup of coffee, which stung her lip just a little, had then dressed and was now in town, shopping for groceries, as Sean had told her to. She had gone in by bus, because she couldn't drive. Sean had never wanted her to learn either.

People naturally looked at her face, but Carol didn't pay any attention. It was humiliating, but Carol was used to it, and she didn't even care what they thought anymore anyway. None of them were going to help her, so why should she care what they thought? But it didn't stop other peoples' looks from getting her down. Apart from the bruises spoiling what would otherwise be a very pretty face she actually looked very nice. She always worked on her appearance. Carol had her dignity.

She wore a beige, acrylic jumper with a round neck, out of which poked a neatly-folded white collar, a blouse underneath, and a light-brown, dark red and white pleated tartan skirt, which came down to just above her knees. The colours were not at all bland on her, they blended and went well together and they made her remarkable auburn hair stand out even more. Funny how not many people chose to notice that truly dazzling natural gift. Considering all the grim factors, she really did look nice. But for Carol, it was difficult to feel it, as the bruises were still there.

She walked alongside a promenade of stores, a snack bar, a charity store, a shoe store, a sports store, and others, carrying her handbag over her shoulder and carrying two bags of shopping, and she walked, quite briskly, to the electronic crossing and pressed the button.

Her stop was just over the road and her bus was there. The 119 to Kingswood. Kingswood was an area of Bedford, where Carol had lived ever since leaving home. Her not too great childhood had been spent in another area of Bedford, Shepherd's Hill, which wasn't far from Kingswood. But there were one or two areas in Bedford, which more or less neighboured one another, like Putnoe and Brickhill for example, although Carol had been to neither of those.

'Shit,' she said to herself, in half a mind to walk straight into the oncoming traffic and go for her bus. 'Come on, damn it.' She had a definite feeling she was going to miss it.

The queue was short and getting shorter. The crossing took an eternity to bleep into action and the traffic came to a halt. But the queue had more or less gone by now and the bus was going to pull away, as soon as the crossing was free and the traffic moved on. People got in her way. She ran as fast as the shopping bags would allow her, along the crossing and down the other side.

There was a row of establishments there too; a food market, a store, a hi-fi dealers and a small branch of a bank, which she was about to go past – at a pretty speedy pace. If anyone was to come out of there, there was a chance that she would collide into them.

The traffic at the crossing was moving again and her bus was about to move off with them, as Carol came almost level with the bank entrance. Someone was already coming out of it; a man, quite tall, and Carol was still running for the bus, but knowing deep down that she wasn't going to make it. They were going to collide. And it was going to be very embarrassing.

Carol didn't realise that the man was directly in her path when she collided with him, so she definitely had no chance to get out of his way. There really wasn't any hurry, but in Carol's mind, that didn't matter. With Sean, she had come to expect the unexpected.

The collision was enough to knock the bags out of Carol's hand, but it was more through surprise than physical force. She had half expected the man to attack her simply for colliding with him, but of course, he didn't.

Some of the bags' contents fell onto the pathway and Carol immediately bent down to retrieve them. She knew that people were looking at her, unable to help staring at her unfortunate collision with the man, but they walked on without giving it much attention. It was no big deal.

But the man with whom she had collided with did not walk on. He stayed to help.

'I'm sorry,' he said. 'Are you okay?'

'Yes, I'm fine thank you,' Carol replied, hastily, but politely, picking up and replacing the groceries into the bags.

'Here, let me help you,' the man said, crouching down to help her.

'No, it's all right, really, I can manage,' Carol said, edgily this time.

Her hurried, hasty manner and the way she spoke no doubt puzzled the man. He was probably also wondering why she never looked up at him. But she dared not do that. He seemed quite nice, but she simply had to get home.

Her bus had already driven by and gone without her. Carol looked at it, disappointedly. 'Damn it,' she said.

'Was that your bus?'

'Yes,' Carol said, and picked up the last few items.

'Never mind, just get the next one.'

'But I wanted that—'

Suddenly looking up at him like that was probably only a natural, instinctive thing to do, or maybe she was just meant to, but as soon as she did – their eyes locked, and it was the sexiest, most powerful, exciting, exhilarating, unforgettable, and frightening feeling that Carol had ever had in her entire life.

The man was initially puzzled by her hurried, hasty manner and in the way she spoke. She seemed very nervous about something. And he was also curious and perhaps more than a little intrigued as to why she didn't look up at him. But when she did look up, he understood why.

He saw the bruises on her face of course, but he ignored them as soon as he'd seen them, since unpleasant feelings of anger, hatred and sympathy threatened to explode inside him and overcome him and he didn't want that. This moment was far too special to spoil it with that. He was only interested in what was behind the bruises. So in a second they were gone. She was the most beautiful woman he'd ever seen. Those lovely grey eyes nearly knocked him sideways; the second their eyes had locked when she looked up had delighted him. It was the most wonderfully uplifting feeling he'd ever had. And, Christ! He noticed the hair!

Something else that he'd noticed too. Even before the bruises. He had seen her hand first. She was wearing a wedding ring.

Carol was instantly scared.

There was a powerful attraction. It only lasted a second, (although it seemed longer), but it was enough. She sensed it. His eyes were a lovely, friendly brown, but she quickly looked away from him, terrified by what she had felt in that instant. Her heart leapt so high, it practically leapt right out of her mouth. And she couldn't begin to explain the amazing somersault her stomach had just made.

She panicked slightly and grabbed her bags, the contents safely back inside again.

She got back up.

'Hey, are you okay?' the man asked again, getting up with her.

'Yes, I'm fine,' Carol insisted, nervously.

People still continued to walk by them, back and forth. Traffic buzzed by, but didn't drown out their voices. The crossing tone back there bleeped into action once again.

'When is your next bus due?' the man asked.

Carol just looked at him. Again, she found herself looking into those kind brown eyes.

'In about ten or fifteen minutes, why?' She felt a shyness

looking up at him, which she didn't really want him to see.

'Well I was wondering. Half the reason you missed that bus was because of me,' the man said.

'I wouldn't have caught it anyway.'

'Maybe, we'll never know that now. I would like to offer you a lift home myself though. It would save you having to queue for another bus. It wouldn't be any trouble.'

Carol suddenly felt and no doubt looked very anxious, edgy, and confused. She tried desperately hard to ignore the attraction she felt towards him, but it was so difficult. Carol wasn't sure if she could ignore it. Or if she should. Terrifying as it may be to admit, after having a moment to think about it, it felt good.

Sean's image loomed in the back of her mind.

'Please?' he said, his kind eyes becoming gently persuasive.

Carol was still very anxious, scared and confused, but there was something about him. About her as well. About this whole thing. It was like a part of herself she didn't even realise she had lost had managed to float to the surface. A response to her genuine sexual appeal. Something like it had happened about four years ago, but this was different. It was like a long-hidden, but glorious re-awakening of something inside her, of someone whom she once felt like. Only somehow, this was even more special. It was like there was a peculiar gentle innocence about it, which she found enormously appealing. Carol considered his offer. And again, she liked it.

Oh, why not, Carol thought. *It was better than waiting for another bus. He could probably get her home a lot quicker anyway.*

'All right,' she said. 'Thank you.'

'My pleasure.'

She was about to go with him to his car. She was still in a great hurry to get home.

'Hold on, just a moment,' he said, stopping.

Carol just looked up at him.

'I was just on my way to grab a bite to eat. So before we go, would you like to join me?'

Carol sensed where this was going and alarm bells began to go off wildly in her head. In the back of her mind too, Sean's image stood, scowling jealously, menacingly clenching his fists, dark eyes glowering. That was the image. But the threat was very real.

'I'm married,' she said, bluntly and with great urgency.

He smiled, gently. 'I know you are. I saw the wedding ring on your finger. When you were picking up your shopping. A bite to eat won't hurt will it? I promise I'll give you a lift home straight afterwards,' he declared.

Carol just looked at him, feeling so many things, and she was shaking. If Sean ever found out that she had had lunch with another man, there was no telling what he would do – he would probably kill her, something which he had come close to doing a couple of times in the past with the abuse and violence, but this time he'd make sure of it. There was no telling the consequences. This could push Sean over the edge, make him even more dangerous. The possibility of that terrified her. What if he saw them together? He was working, so the chances of that happening were very slim, but there was still a chance. There was always a chance.

But Carol couldn't help but like this man. The attraction just a moment ago had terrified her because it was so strong, even in that split second. But perhaps that was it; the fact that she was attracted to another man, who was also attracted to her, the thrill she got from it was deep down still exciting even if it was terrifying because of the very real consequences that went with it. Perhaps that was why the attraction felt so strong. She couldn't help but like him however – that fact was impossible to ignore, even with Sean's threatening image in the back of her mind, haunting her, as if he was keeping an eye on her without even being here. Daring her to make a move.

She kept looking at the man. His brown eyes were kind and sincere and she liked his smile. He didn't push her, he was just gently persuasive. He didn't really need to be.

Yes, she really liked him. His quite longish, neatly styled medium-light-brown hair, his undominative six-foot-one-inch frame. (He was a couple of inches taller than Sean.) He wore a light suit, white shirt and tie. He was slim, but not skinny. He wasn't handsome, more attractive; he had a nice, oblong face, which was in fact rather colourless, just a tiny hint of colour stopped him from being almost pale, and a weak, but soft chin and jaw-line. She was still looking into his eyes.

'Please. I promise, straight home afterwards.'

A mild, thankful half-smile lifted Carol's mouth, to her surprise. 'Okay, just a bite to eat,' she said, and almost immediately, in response, her heart settled into a wonderfully exciting, fast-beating rhythm, possibly in anticipation of what might happen.

'Great.'

They walked on together.

'By the way,' he said. 'I'm Greg Thompson.' He held out his hand.

Carol smiled. It was a genuine smile this time. Where was it coming from all of a sudden? She did it without thinking. She shook his hand, gladly. It was also soft. 'Carol Davis,' she said.

'Nice to meet you, Carol.'

'You too,' Carol said with another smile.

'Hey, let me help you with one of those,' Greg said.

He took a bag off her before she could do anything. She didn't bother trying to stop him anyway.

'Thank you,' she said.

They smiled at each other and walked on.

The image of Sean in Carol's mind had now faded for the time being. In fact, through the excitement, she wasn't even thinking about it, and she hadn't even realised it.

The two of them ate sandwiches, crisps and drank coffee at a busy snack bar which wasn't that far from where they had had their mishap.

They sat on opposite sides of a white plastic table, and were very much in good conversation with each other. They looked to be thoroughly enjoying each other's company, and Carol was visibly all smiles. She enjoyed it.

They were leaning towards each other, arms resting loosely on the table, and even their hands were flat down on the table, quite close together too, as if they wanted to touch, except for when they made natural movements during conversation. So their body language spoke for itself.

Carol had also managed to laugh on a few occasions. She hadn't even realised that she hadn't done something as simple as that in a very long time either.

They continued chatting, whilst in the background, people continued to move along the self-service bar, picking up hot snacks, crisps, desserts and chocolate bars, while the pretty blonde cashier at the end totted up their bills. All kinds of hot snack odours drifted through the air, plus the clatter and rustle of the people still getting their snacks and the pleasant rhythmic hum of the coffee machine. The chatter of people at other tables added to the cosy, rather casual mood.

Carol had never felt so relaxed and happy in all her life than now whilst she was talking to Greg. She was relishing his company. It was like talking to an old friend, even though she'd barely met the guy. And Sean had been wiped completely out of her mind. Something she never thought would happen.

She sat cross-legged. She let her shoe dangle from her toes. She ran a hand smoothly back over her auburn hair and pushed it gently behind her ear. She was enjoying herself.

However, not once during their entire conversation did Greg mention or ask about the bruises on her face, so therefore, Carol had actually forgotten all about them. People in the snack bar had looked at her and from the disgusted expressions on their faces, she knew what they were thinking, and by the even more disgusted way they had looked at Greg, it was obvious that they even thought Greg was responsible for inflicting them. Something which actually amused her.

You have absolutely no idea, Carol had thought to herself, wryly. *The bruises are half the reason why I'm here with him.*

Instead of sitting there feeling embarrassed, or indeed feeling sorry for Greg about the totally false way in which he was being seen, although it didn't seem to bother him – (something she didn't even think he was capable of doing), she found herself enjoying the attention for once. Being seen with Greg maintained her excitement. Her anticipation of what was to happen was also tantalised even more. After a few moments of talking to him though, she forgot all about that.

While they were talking, she also noticed how the expressions on some of the people at nearby tables had changed, to wry amusement. From the way she was seemingly flirting with Greg, maybe they realised now that their initial assumptions had been wrong. And were amused about what she was doing.

Then, sometime later, when the chat suddenly had a chance to mellow down, it gave Greg a chance to realise the time, and the shock of it was enough to cut him off completely.

'Good God, we've been here for over an hour,' Greg said, glancing down at his watch. 'Sorry, I hadn't realised.'

'Jesus, an hour,' Carol said, she too surprised at the time, but it didn't scare her into a panic like she thought it might have done.

'Oh, well, come on then, I'll give you that lift home I promised you.'

Her enthusiasm now was less than bright.

'Okay, thanks,' Carol said, flatly. The glowing, smiling face that had practically beamed during their lunch had disappeared altogether, to be replaced by a more forlorn, disappointed look. Disappointment that her time with Greg had come to an end. And of course the reality of Sean invading her mind once again.

Now that that realisation had come upon her, Sean's image was well and truly back in her mind. More terrifying than before. Not surprisingly, he looked furious, albeit only a vision in her mind. He looked like he would kill her. Going behind his back. Seeing another man. Even though he really had no way of knowing.

Carol had suddenly become terribly confused and depressed. She knew she wanted to be with Greg, she really liked him, but being married to Sean made it impossible. He was capable of such horrendous violence and abuse. But the thought of being with Sean and never seeing Greg again, was horrible. She didn't really want to be taken home. She wanted to be with him. She wanted to go home with him. Why couldn't she have met Greg before? In short, this was beginning to become a complicated mess, and in such a short space of time.

'Hey,' Greg said, as they were getting up, 'are you all right?'

Carol made the best smile she could, but it was not very convincing. She nodded.

'Where's that lovely smiling face I love disappeared to?'

They put their trays on the pile on their way out of the snack bar.

'I smiled just then didn't I?'

'The one before practically *glowed.*'

'Sorry.'

'No, don't be sorry. I just wondered why you looked so miserable all of a sudden. I didn't mean to upset you. I thought you wanted a lift home.'

Carol could not help but wonder if Greg was playing some kind of a game here with her. Surely he knew what was going on. Surely he knew where the bruises came from. He hadn't mentioned them once up to now and Carol was very grateful for that. It was very considerate, but not bringing them up now when it was so obvious that he had noticed them and might even be curious about them, seemed to be almost evasive somehow. But she didn't detect any insincerity in his voice. None at all. And she had no reason not to trust him. In fact, she suspected that he was avoiding the subject deliberately, allowing it to rumble menacingly under the surface of their attraction. The hidden threat actually made it far more thrilling for them than if it was brought right out into the open.

'I do want a lift,' Carol said. 'It's just that… oh, forget it, it doesn't matter.'

'No, please, tell me,' Greg said. 'It'll bother me for the rest of the day if you don't.'

As they walked, Carol looked up at him. 'It's just that… I was rather enjoying talking to you in there, that's all.'

Carol saw Greg's smile, just before she looked away from him and carried on walking. She was rather embarrassed with herself for admitting that, and walked with a brisker pace.

'Yes, I enjoyed talking to you too,' Greg said. 'You're very good company.'

She gave him a quick, glancing grin.

'So much so, that I'd like to see you again. And the sooner the better as well.'

'No, Greg. That's nice of you, but I don't think that's a good idea.'

'Why?'

Carol began to walk even faster, her heartbeat accelerating again, terrified of where this was going.

Greg's car wasn't too far away now. He'd said it was parked a little way down the road. Greg had no problem keeping up with her.

Brief panic once more.

'Why don't you think it's a good idea, Carol?'

'Because… because I just don't, that's all.'

'Hey, if we enjoy each other's company so much, of course it's a good idea.'

'Greg, you said a bite to eat and then you'd take me home. So, please, can we just go to your car?'

Carol was still speeding up, her walk had become very brisk. But Greg still found it quite easy to keep up with her. They neared his car.

'I know I said that,' Greg said, 'but that was before I found out what charming company I was with.'

'It's still not a good idea, Greg, and you know it.'

Carol was terrified at the idea of cheating on Sean. The anticipation of what could happen with Greg had been exciting, especially during their lunch together when she didn't have to think about anything else, now all she could think about was where it would eventually lead to with Sean involved. She would never be able to go behind his back and get away with it. She wasn't sure she even wanted to.

They were almost at his car. She walked fast, almost jogging. But Carol knew she wouldn't be able to escape this conversation even when they got to his car.

'I don't see why. Why isn't it?' Greg asked, still very calm.

Carol suddenly stopped, turned and looked straight up at him. 'Because I'm married, Greg. Okay? I'm *married*.'

Greg looked straight back at her. Carol felt a slight shudder as their eyes locked again. He was so calm. For a second, very briefly, possibly a moment of sexual excitement, she couldn't help but wonder what his body was like. He was slim obviously, gentle and possibly very soft. Another quiver of embarrassment rippled in her stomach.

She felt a sadness inside her, wondering why she had to meet Greg under these circumstances. It was totally unfair. She had had hopes and dreams of escaping the violence at home, but she never expected this. This was even more difficult. She also knew that she was only using being married as a cover, to hide her fears of where this was going and her sudden feelings for Greg.

'I know that, Carol. I saw your ring, remember. And I admit, I do feel a little guilty about seeing another man's wife.' Carol couldn't help but wonder if that was a lie or not. Maybe he did feel just as guilty as her. But was it guilt, or was it fear for him too, since he knew what he was getting into?

'But the attraction between us was very strong and we're good together.'

With a frustrated sigh, Carol walked off, Greg followed and they arrived at his car, a dark blue Ford Orion.

Carol went to the passenger side of Greg's car, grabbed the door handle and stood there.

Greg approached her, a hand in his trouser pocket. 'I'm sorry if this is confusing you, Carol, but I really do want to see you again. And I'm positive that you want the same.'

Carol swallowed. Her heart was thundering.

'Could we get in please'?' she said, woodenly, looking the other way, avoiding any eye-contact. The last thing she needed right now was to look into those brown eyes of his.

For a moment, she actually felt pleasantly intimidated (like feeling another brief sexual thrill), as he stood almost right behind her on the pavement, while she waited by the passenger door, holding onto the handle.

Greg remained calm, casual, he just kept looking at her. She felt his warm gaze. 'I'll put your bags in the boot first,' he said, and took his keys from out of his trouser pocket. He put them in the boot of his car and then went to the driver's side, unlocked it and got in. Carol followed, getting in beside him. A sudden, curious feeling of cosiness settled through her as she sat there in the passenger seat, putting on her seat-belt. Jesus, her emotions were playing havoc.

As Greg put on his own seat-belt, he said; 'You know, I really do miss that glowing smile you had in the snack bar. Seems a shame to lose it.'

'Greg, I've already told you, I'm married. Can't you understand that? I can't see you again.'

This was agony. She knew she wanted to see him again, but she was scared, and she was still using the marriage as a cover, to hide her own fears.

Sitting here in the car next to Greg as he got ready to drive her home, she knew exactly where she was going, but at the same time, she felt so lost, and her real destination couldn't be more uncertain. She felt like asking him to drive back to his place and never have to face this again. But she didn't.

'Okay,' he said, sounding rather bold, 'forget about *can't*. Do you want me to see you again?'

Carol couldn't respond. The only genuine response to that was an unquestionable and resounding, Yes! But she couldn't say it. Her tongue had locked, her mouth made no effort to form the word. It stayed inside her, imprisoned by her fear. She breathed deeply.

'Carol, please, look at me.'

Oh, God, no. She couldn't. She didn't. She turned the opposite way from him and looked out the window, folding her arms tightly. Her legs were crossed. If she looked at him, she would have to look into his wonderful brown eyes again. And it felt too good to look into them.

'Please, Carol, look at me,' he said again.

She blinked nervously, several times. Her heart was thumping ferociously. Possibly excitedly. She knew there was something good between them, and she was so attracted to Greg, but she was frightened to admit it to herself, because of Sean. His threatening presence in the background still terrified her. She was going to have to tell him about Greg sooner or later, so eventually he would find out. There was even a tiny hint of guilt inside her for being happy with Greg. Sean was still her husband.

'Carol, I'm sorry to have to say this, but I'm not driving until you do.'

Jesus, now what? Carol was amazed at his bravery. But she needed a hard bargain like that to make her say it. Damn him for handling this so well. For helping her to confront her own feelings.

Carol could feel her eyes building up with tears of sadness and frustration.

'Carol…'

She finally did so very quickly, before she could change her mind – looking directly into his eyes.

It was like a spell. She immediately felt herself being drawn in by those delicious pools of brown. She was so attracted to him, but she was terrified of where it would lead; of what would happen if she surrendered to the attraction, of where her feelings would take her if she did allow herself to surrender and accept whatever dangerous or unpleasant consequences that came with it. After living a life of violence and abuse for so long, right now, the consequences of this scared her even more. The violence was something she had almost learned to live with.

'What do you want me to say?' Carol asked.

'Just whatever you feel,' Greg replied simply.

Carol kept her eyes on his. She wasn't able to look away. Her heart was in overdrive. Nervous, fluttery waves were rippling up through her stomach and all the way up through her body. She could even feel a tear about to fall.

Greg's expression wasn't at all demanding. He simply sat there, waiting for her answer. He really was going to sit there until she answered. Damn.

She swallowed. Afraid to say what she really wanted to say.

Greg waited. He raised his eyebrows. It made his brown eyes seem bigger.

'Yes,' Carol said finally. If she left it any longer, she wouldn't have been able to say anything. 'I do. Satisfied?'

Greg smiled, appreciatively. No smugness. Obviously, he was just pleased to hear her say it. 'Thank you,' he said, starting the car and putting it into gear.

'For what?'

'For being honest,' Greg said to her, with a grin, and drove off.

Carol wasn't sure if it made her feel any better.

They hadn't been driving for very long at all, when Greg asked; 'So, how about it, can I see you again?'

'I don't know,' Carol replied, distantly, at last giving it some serious thought.

She was still afraid of taking this any further, even though she had told him the truth about wanting to see him again.

She tried to think about what would happen if she did; tried to imagine the consequences before they actually happened. It was difficult to imagine such a thing – it was always hard predicting the future; but the basic outcome was Sean discovering her affair with Greg, and… she closed her eyes tight and leaned her elbow against the very narrow window ledge of her door and rubbed her fingertips on her forehead. The image of Sean's terrifying reaction was too much for her to picture in her mind's eye. She swallowed and clenched her jaw. Anguish and frustration was making her tired.

'You're thinking about Sean, aren't you?' Greg asked, delicately.

She turned to look at him, her expression full of the frustration she felt at not knowing what to do. 'Yes,' she said.

'There must be a way,' Greg said, sounding frustrated himself. He too was obviously desperate to meet up with her again. 'There has to be.'

'Nothing I can think of,' Carol said.

'Surely he can't keep an eye on you twenty-four hours a day.'

'You don't know him.'

'I don't think I want to,' Greg remarked, bitterly.

Carol flashed him a sudden surprised look.

He looked a little angry with himself for letting her in on the way he really felt about Sean. But it was only natural that it was going to come out sooner or later without him realising it. She wasn't stupid, she already knew that's how he felt.

'Jesus. I'm sorry, I didn't mean to say that,' he said.

'It's all right. I knew you'd make a comment about him sooner or later. I'm surprised it's taken you this long.'

'No, I didn't want to say anything about that. It's none of my business.'

'I don't think you believe that anymore than I do.'

'Maybe not.'

Carol didn't say anything for a brief moment. But now that Greg had mentioned it and it was out in the open, Carol didn't want Greg thinking any less of her because of it. There was no reason why he should obviously, but it made no difference. She didn't want to let it go.

She then said; 'He just… he just gets so angry, that's all. He's got this unbelievable temper, and he gets these dark rages inside him that he just can't control. I'm not making excuses for him. It's just the way he is. He used to be really exciting company. I did once love him. Sometimes I wonder if I still do.'

Carol was almost going to say that he didn't do it that often, but that sounded too lame and she was worth more than that and so was Greg, Sean too, come to that.

Greg sighed. 'Yeah,' he said.

It was obvious to Carol that he didn't particularly like the subject and certainly didn't want to talk about it. But she had guessed that even though he remained silent. She also sensed that it was rather difficult for him, even thinking about it and not wanting to say anything.

Carol was surprised he didn't say anything else, but she was grateful.

'Carol, do you mind if we change the subject, please?' Greg said at last. 'We were discussing another meeting.'

'I know,' Carol said. 'I still can't think of anything.'

'Well, surely he goes out on his own sometimes. Out for a drink with his mates or something.'

They came to a set of traffic lights that were red, and Greg stopped. They were now in Kingswood, and it wasn't far to Carol's place.

'Sometimes he does. But he only ever stays out a few hours. We would never have enough time.'

'Well, a few hours is better than nothing,' Greg said. 'I don't live that far away. So, getting there and back wouldn't be a problem.'

The lights changed to green. Greg drove on.

Soon, they were back at Carol's place. She hadn't said anything else yet. Greg pulled up outside her house. It was just after half-one, and Sean wasn't in. Carol had half expected his building company car to be there. With him waiting.

The time seemed to have flown by. An eternity had passed in not much time at all.

Carol was very depressed. This whole thing was really scaring her, and it was getting her down. She still didn't say another word. Greg glanced at her and she felt his sympathy.

'I'll get your bags for you,' he said. They both got out of the car.

He got the bags from out of the boot and handed them to her.

'Thank you,' she said.

Carol felt a slight chill outside in the mild air. She preferred the cosiness of his car.

She walked away, and Greg then walked up to her.

'Carol, we—'

She turned to face him. 'Greg, I'm sorry. I don't know yet. I'll have to think it over. I wasn't expecting any of this.'

'Do you think I was? I'm glad it happened. I really like you, Carol. I want to see you again.'

'And I'm married to Sean, Greg. I'm sorry, but I am. And if he ever found out…'

Greg closed his eyes, obviously not willing to picture it himself either. 'I know,' he said.

'You must understand how much this is scaring me. I need some time to think it over. All right?'

Greg raised his eyebrows, surrendering. He smiled, patiently. 'Sure, I understand,' he said. 'But look, if you do decide, then,' he took a bit of note-paper and a pen from his inside jacket pocket and wrote something down, 'give me a call, okay? This is my home number, no answering-machine, only my business number has one of them, so you're guaranteed to get me or nothing, okay?'

Carol smiled. 'Okay.' She knew the smile was nowhere near as good as the one in the snack bar, but what the hell.

He handed her the paper.

'Thank you,' she said. 'Well, I'd better go inside, I have some cleaning up to do.'

Greg nodded. 'Yeah.'

That short response again made Carol wonder what else he was thinking. But it didn't really matter.

She turned and walked away, with an unconscious, but slight, and very nice-to-look-at swing of her hips.

It was something she was almost instantly aware of. She could feel Greg looking at her from behind and again she became consciously aware of herself, her body and of her sexual appeal.

She could feel him looking at her as she walked, enjoying the gentle, but sensual swing of her hips and the movement of her bottom under her skirt. She could feel him enjoying her pretty legs too, what he could see of them. It made her grin.

It was a glorious awareness inside her. She could feel him enjoying all these thrills and getting all this pleasure out of looking at her. But it was she who was feeling that pleasure of looking good and feeling it. It made her glow inside. And once again, she had forgotten about the bruises on her face.

Her moderately slim, but effeminately cuddly figure, sculpted out well by her jumper and skirt felt warm and snug, but there was always that sliver of cold in the pit of her stomach as she headed for the front door and the unpleasant reality of what was behind it.

She was aware of her bruises again. She also knew that Greg was still looking at her. And of course, she knew he liked her hair. She just knew.

She quickly glanced around once more at Greg and he was indeed standing there by his car, looking after her, grinning, with a hint of sadness. He looked like he wanted to come with her. She wanted him to. She turned back and walked on.

'Carol,' he said suddenly.

She stopped and turned around to face him.

'Think about it. Please.'

Carol sighed. She nodded, reluctantly and battled with a smile, which lost out. Again, she turned back and walked right up to the front door. She took out her key and let herself in. Much as she'd left it, but Carol felt different somehow. As she closed the front door, she looked out once more at Greg, with a hopeful grin and a nod which she hoped wasn't a last goodbye.

Greg wasn't sure whether to feel happy or sad as Carol walked into the house and shut the door, with a quick grin and a nod out to him.

He did feel pretty awful at the moment it had to be said. He couldn't help but wonder if he would ever see her again.

He'd never met anyone like her. She was pleasant, easy-going, undeniably attractive, fun to be with, and even kind of sexy – in her own innocent sort of way. She seemed to have an inner passion too and a special quality which made her even more appealing. But would he ever see her again?

He was quite sure he wanted to take this relationship further. He definitely wanted to see her again. And he was sure that Carol wanted the same thing. But he also thought about, respected and understood her fear of her husband.

It scared him. Would he even see her again alive?

With a deep breath of disbelief at such a thought, he got back into his car, but didn't immediately drive off.

Greg sat there behind the wheel, beginning to breathe heavily. His heart began to accelerate, and an anger began to rise up inside him. All those negative emotions that threatened to attack and overwhelm him when he first saw her were returning with a vengeance. Tears glittered in his eyes and he had an urge to shout at the top of his voice. His hands gripped the steering wheel so hard, his knuckles whitened.

Suddenly, he released his grip on the steering wheel and began to beat his fists onto it; both at the same time, then the left, then the right, left, right, both at the same time. Tears spilled from his eyes. He beat his fists on the steering wheel; left, right, both at the same time. Alone with his thoughts, after having them kept in for a while, he needed the release.

The way Greg felt about Carol, in only the instant he'd known her, made it very painful indeed to know the sort of treatment she was getting at the hands of Sean. The treatment he was giving her behind closed doors filled Greg with the darkest feelings he could imagine. Beaten and abused, probably to the point of screaming for mercy. He just couldn't understand him.

Married, Carol had said on a few occasions.

Married was not the word for it. This wasn't a marriage. It was nothing of the kind. It was really nothing but a convenient weapon for Sean's violence.

Greg's own parents were still married. Happily. Alan and Patricia Thompson. He could remember from when he was young, how much in love they were. He wasn't afraid to admit it either. Or say it. He'd witnessed them making love with each other one night by the fire, when he was only seven. It'd been a very strange experience for him, but not at all damaging. But having lived with happy parents like that, it was even more hurtful to know what was happening to Carol. It was a struggle to handle it for sure. And he certainly wasn't at all tough by any means. He just had to pray it was going to work out.

He stopped hitting the steering wheel. He wiped his eyes. He started the car and drove off, hoping that he and Carol Davis would be seeing each other again soon.

Carol felt more anxious than afraid.

Sean arrived home from work at just after seven. The house was nice and tidy and Carol had his tea already prepared. But her mind hadn't been fully concentrating on it this evening, because she was half-thinking about Greg, and of the events earlier this afternoon, even though she tried desperately hard not to. And as a result, she had burnt the fish fillets she had planned on serving him. Sean was in a foul mood anyway – so yet again, Carol was forced to endure Sean's violence.

She was slapped around for what seemed like hours, though it was nowhere near that long.

But the violence she was used to. What she wasn't used to was wondering if she could indeed put a stop to this. Was there a way to get herself out of the violence?

After being with a wonderful, kind and gentle man, like Greg, earlier this afternoon – someone who really made her feel good, (like Sean used to), the violence all over again almost made it seem like Greg had never existed to start with; he was a cruel fantasy, a figure of happiness, a pleasure man who was gone, out of her life forever. There was also a hint of embarrassment for Carol too. She had not been very open with Greg after he had brought her back, now she was suffering this again. She hated herself for that. And could Sean tell if she'd been up to something? Could he see it in her eyes? He'd suspected her of all kinds of things in the past, but those times she'd been innocent. Not this time. It was almost as if he was hitting her like this because he knew what was going on.

All kinds of things buzzed around in her mind.

She also wondered if she would be able to survive tonight.

She hoped Sean would be at work tomorrow, but that would mean she probably wouldn't be able to get hold of Greg, as he'd be working as well. She wondered if she would ever see him again. So many thoughts. So many concerns.

But right now, she had to get through this. Sean still wasn't finished. She tried to run away this time, screaming at him to stop, but he would only pull her back, become more angry, and hit her even harder. The slaps then turned into punches again. One, then another to her stomach, another to her jaw. Not as bad as it could have been, or could be, but Carol was desperately hoping that he wouldn't do too much damage, like break a tooth or something, as that would spoil or at least change the face of the attractive woman that Greg had been with earlier.

She went down again. Not for the first time.

'Bloody, stupid irritating bitch!' Sean yelled down at her. 'Have I gotta come home to this every night?'

Sean then took it out on the kitchen itself and the crockery, still managing to scare Carol, who thought there was more to come for her, as she lay there in anticipation of being hit or kicked again. He knocked the plates off the table, sending them smashing across the floor, and the cutlery too, which made eerie tinkling sounds as it scattered across the tiles. He grabbed a couple of cups and smashed them too, then he kicked the dining table chairs, sending them screeching across the floor.

Carol, who was still lying on the floor, tucked up against a cupboard door, swore he was going to kick her too, but he didn't, which was a minor relief.

Sean then stormed off to the hallway to get his jacket and grab her handbag from the peg. He pulled out her purse and took a couple of notes out. Two tens by the look of it. Well, like he would say, he did earn it.

Carol peered at him through her dishevelled hair, which still looked alive, but obviously untidy. For the first time, there was a little anger in her expression, although Sean couldn't see it. He came into the kitchen again and looked at her.

'I'm off to the pub to get something to eat,' he growled. 'I can't stay 'ere a minute longer.' He still looked fired up with anger. He looked at the broken crockery on the floor. 'And I want that mess cleaned up before I get back. I don't wanna have to come back to that too.'

He left, angrily, and Carol heard the front door slam shut. She couldn't help but cry now she was alone, the presence of Sean no longer looming over her.

But there were several other things that were on her mind. And one way or another, they all scared her.

Carol cleaned up the broken crockery and everything else. She lay there for a few moments, uncertain, anxious, and afraid, before getting up to do so, but after cleaning it up, she then went to the hallway, and her heart sank when she remembered where she had put Greg's phone number. Her handbag. In a moment of instinctive panic, she reached in and grabbed it. Christ, Sean could've found it and then what would've happened?

She didn't think about it. She was just pleased it was still there, tucked down at the bottom. She took it out and looked at it, nursing her face. The need to call him became overpowering. She had to. She convinced herself that she wasn't just running to him for protection. She genuinely wanted to see him again.

It felt strange to be able to call him. Before, she had never had this luxury. It was almost as if she felt she didn't deserve it. As if it couldn't really happen. The anxiety and uncertainty was still swimming roughly around inside her, and its insistent, almost angry white surfs were constantly beating against her.

The violence stopping and starting again and again, was like a vicious circle – only this time, she had been given a break in the circle, someone she could be with who she wanted to be with. A loving shoulder. It felt very strange. This break in the circle filled her with fear almost as much as her previous day to day life of violence had done, and it was mostly because of the consequences of what could happen afterwards.

She had to do it. It was now or never. She had nothing to lose.

She licked her sore lips, took a deep breath, which hurt a little and then picked up the phone. She dialled.

'Oh, God, please be home, please,' she whispered to herself as it rang.

She was about to think he would never answer after only six

rings, but then his unmistakable and much welcomed voice clicked on. 'Hello?'

A flood of relief washed through her, seeming to cleanse all her wounds. She smiled, instinctively.

'Hi, Greg, it's Carol.'

The enthusiasm in his voice on the other end was also unmistakable, and wonderful to hear.

'Carol!' he said loudly. 'I never expected to hear from you so soon.'

'I never thought I'd be calling so soon.'

'It's great to hear your voice again.'

'It's good to hear yours too.'

There was a brief silence. Only a few seconds.

Carol then said; 'I want to see you again.'

Greg puffed with relief. 'Jesus, I thought I'd never hear you say that. You don't know how good that is to hear, Carol.' He then said; 'Where's Sean gone?'

'Does it matter?'

'I'll admit, I am interested.'

'He's gone to the pub for something to eat. Dinner didn't go too well. I burnt it. Too busy thinking about you. He was in a bad mood anyway.'

'I'm glad, funnily enough.'

'I actually thought he knew about what happened this afternoon.'

'Did he?'

'No,' Carol said with an ironic grunt.

'Well, no point in wasting time. Shall I come and pick you up?'

'Yes, please,' Carol said. 'Thank you.'

'Okay. I shouldn't be long. Give me about fifteen minutes, all right? I'll be there as soon as possible.'

'Okay, I'll be waiting. Impatiently.'

Greg chuckled. 'Okay. See you soon.'

'Thanks, bye.'

'Bye for now.' He hung up.

Good, he was on his way.

Carol put the phone down and grabbed her handbag, as if it was a lifeline, putting Greg's number back inside it.

Before waiting for him in the lounge, she went upstairs to the bathroom to wash her face, bathe her fresh wounds, and brush her hair, which, with all that was going on, still retained a wonderful vitality. She checked herself over, excitedly, and went back downstairs.

She sat in the lounge on the sofa, hunched forward, and carefully hugging herself. Right now, she didn't feel much pain. She felt anxious and even more scared.

Seeing Greg again – actually doing so. It was unbelievable. She sat there, shaking with fear and anticipation. But hidden deep inside her, almost afraid to come to the surface, was that strange excitement of going ahead with it and seeing him that gave her such a secret thrill. This was all so weird. There was also a bizarre fear that Sean would walk back in any second – unexpectedly, which made the wait so long, anxious and scary.

But again, it was strangely exciting too.

It seemed like forever, waiting for Greg to arrive, but he did so after about fourteen minutes. He knocked on the front door three times, sounding just as impatient as Carol was.

Carol was up like a shot with her handbag and went to the front door. She tucked her hair back and stood up straight, ready to greet him, and then she opened it, and Greg stood there, looking very chic in a white shirt and dark trousers, up against the clear evening sky.

'Hi there,' he said. He looked as if he noticed the fresh marks on her face, but chose to ignore them. 'Ready?'

Carol nodded, with a smile. Her heart had already leapt with excitement. The anticipation of what was to come was now stronger than ever. She was turned on by simply looking up at him. At six-one, he was two inches taller than Sean, but nowhere near as big or strong in build, and looking up at his delicious brown eyes was even better.

'Then let's go,' Greg said, grinning.

Carol walked out to him, closed the door behind her and quickly followed Greg out to his car. They both moved quite briskly, knowing time was important and not to be wasted. Carol still looked out for Sean.

When they were both in the car, Carol's heart was still thumping. She felt nervous, excited, scared, anxious, thrilled; it was a whole mixture of feelings, one followed by another, whirling dizzily around inside her – in fact, much as she'd felt all day, ever since meeting Greg and that initial attraction. God, it was all so weird.

'I can't believe this you know,' Carol said. 'It feels so weird. I can't believe I'm actually doing this.'

Greg looked at her with a smile as he started the car up.

'Feels good though, doesn't it?'

Carol looked at him and smiled. 'Yes, I suppose it does.'

'That's all I care about.'

Carol was still looking at him, mostly out the corner of her eye. And Greg glanced across at her as he drove off, probably knowing that she was still looking at him and that's when Carol smiled at him once again, and Greg smiled back, but this time, he looked pleased, and Carol immediately realised that her smile was glowing as it did before. She could almost feel it, and she was delighted.

As they drove off, Carol looked around once to see if Sean was behind them, but there was no one, and Carol turned back and faced forward again, and she felt both terrified and excited and also relieved, as they gradually left her house behind.

She wasn't sure whether to smile or cry.

They arrived at Greg's place at about a quarter to eight. He lived a few miles outside of Kingswood, in a small village, called Ridgely. Carol was expecting a posh flat, as she knew he had no family, but he actually lived in his own house, by himself of course, possibly with the hope that maybe he might have his own family one day. It was a nice place, smaller than hers, detached, with flat windows and a white painted front door, which had a small window at the centre. It had that pleasant, quiet, no fuss village look, but it was also modern. Carol realised Greg wasn't short of a few pounds, but then again, neither was Sean. Builders' earnings were high.

Greg pulled into the small gravel driveway and they both got out. Carol looked at his house with admiration.

'You have a nice place,' she said.

'Thank you, but don't be completely fooled, Carol, my mum

and dad both helped to pay for it.'

Carol smiled, wryly and they both walked up to the front door and Greg let them in.

The inside was warmly welcoming. The hallway was darkly carpeted, with beige walls on which small prints were hung, mostly of flowers. A small table was set with a china pot of flowers. His phone was there too.

'Come on through to the lounge,' Greg said.

'Okay.'

They walked in, Greg first clicking on the light, and Carol looked around briefly. There was a large television set with video-recorder in the corner, near the window; and the entire spread was a cosy mixture of brown and light colours. Deep-pile creme-brown carpet, beige walls again and a deep, chocolate-brown leather suite, and some china ornaments decorated the window sill and the mantelpiece.

There was a dark wood wall unit at the end, down from the fireplace, with a small drinks cabinet. A display cabinet and a stereo-stack was next to that, in the middle.

'Very nice,' Carol said again.

'Thank you. Would you like a drink?'

Carol stood there, puzzling over it for a few seconds and said; 'Yes, I think I will. Do you have anything light?'

'Light?' He opened the drinks cabinet and took out a half-full bottle of Martini. 'You mean like this?'

Carol smiled and nodded. 'That'll be fine, thanks.'

'Please, sit down, make yourself at home,' Greg said, as he poured the two of them a glass.

Carol sat on the end of the sofa, furthest from the television, dropped her handbag beside it and crossed her legs. She leaned her head back and closed her eyes. A deep sigh escaped her.

It felt strange being here now, now that that particular sense of anticipation had passed. She was here now. All she had to do from here was to try and settle down.

Greg came with their drinks. 'There you go,' he said.

Carol opened her eyes and took her drink. 'Thank you,' she said.

Greg walked across and sat next to her on the sofa. He didn't sit too close, but he didn't sit right at the other end of the sofa either, as if they'd had a serious argument. Instead, Greg sat more near the middle, holding his drink.

The room might have been a little dead without the television on, or without a fire burning, and no music on either. But Carol liked it that way. The atmosphere was calm and friendly, with a pleasant sincerity to it that made Carol feel instantly at home. But there was still some uncertainty. She didn't really know why. Maybe it was because this was still all so strange and now she had to make it work.

Greg still sat there, not saying a word yet. Carol wondered what he was doing, as she was still sitting there with her head laid back and her eyes closed. But she didn't bother opening them to take a look. Not yet. She also hoped that he didn't mind her sitting here so quiet like this. Maybe he was just sitting there looking at her, which she liked.

Greg's voice then broke the peaceful, comfortable silence, although Carol wouldn't have minded him sitting there, peacefully looking at her all evening to be honest.

'You know, I can't tell you how pleased I was when I got your call,' he said.

Carol opened her eyes again and looked at him. He was grinning back at her. He had been sitting there looking after all.

'As soon as I got in – I confess, I waited for the phone to ring. I couldn't stop thinking about you.'

No particular reaction from Carol, she just looked at him.

'Yes, I know, it sounds corny. But it's the truth.'

Carol looked down at her untouched drink. She was slightly embarrassed, but not that much. She really was beginning to warm to Greg's affections.

'Yes, I couldn't stop thinking about you either. Why do you think I ruined me and Sean's dinner?'

'When do you think Sean will be back?' Greg asked.

'I don't know,' Carol replied. 'But he won't be that long. I'd say about a few hours.'

'Pity he couldn't stay out all night,' Greg said, half joking, and sipping his drink.

Carol grunted. 'Wouldn't surprise me if he did,' she said quietly, mostly to herself.

'Really? Why's that?'

Carol glanced at him. 'Oh, he'd probably chat up a girl there, take her back home to her place and have sex with her.'

'He'd do that?'

Carol grinned, wryly. 'I don't know. Hard to tell sometimes what Sean is capable of. As I say, it wouldn't surprise me. But I'd take no chances. What if he did get home soon?'

'Yes, of course. Although, I do find it hard to imagine that a woman would be attracted to a man like that,' he added. 'No offence.'

Carol grinned. 'None taken. A lot of women do like guys like Sean, believe it or not. It's some kind of animal magnetism, I don't know. That's what attracted me anyway. He used to be exciting company.'

Carol drank some of her Martini. Greg did so too.

'I suppose we'll just have to make use of the time we've got then.'

'Yes,' Carol said simply, although underneath, she was a little saddened about them not having much time to spend together, and she supposed that Greg felt much the same.

'Hey, don't look so depressed, Carol, we do have some time together.'

Carol laughed a little. 'Sorry.'

'That's better. There's that smile I love so much.'

She looked at him. Her heart fluttered and something pleasant flipped over in her stomach. She wasn't used to hearing such nice things. For nearly three years (although it'd seemed like a hell of a lot longer), she had listened to Sean's foul, vicious abuse; insulting her, putting her down, telling her she couldn't do anything right. All of it was stored in the back of her mind, along with the hideous memories of violence and sexual assault, and the humiliation of going to the hospital to repair damage to her body. Not to mention the degrading reactions of people outside to the bruises on her face.

She remembered the two doctors' comments at the hospital on one occasion about the bruising to her back, arms and the ones on her jaw – she had said it'd been a mugging and a recent accident, nothing to worry about. Eventually, she had told them, after several beating-around-the-bush questions, that it was not their concern – what else could she do? Besides, she wasn't really in a position to care what they were thinking. That would have been a luxury.

'Hey,' Greg said, 'it's a bit dead in here, isn't it? How about I get a fire burning?'

'Yes, okay,' Carol said. She didn't mind that.

'Then how about the TV or some music in the background?'

'No, no TV thanks. I'm not in the mood. And I'd prefer it silent, if you wouldn't mind.'

'No, I don't mind. Well, I'll get that fire burning anyhow.'

As Greg began to get a fire going, Carol said; 'I can't believe I'm here you know. It seems like a dream. And maybe I'll wake up and see Sean standing there over me.'

Greg glanced back at her. 'Carol, you're here because you want to be. Not because someone twisted your arm and forced you into it. I know I didn't, so my conscience is clear,' he said, glancing back at her with a smile.

Carol just grinned. 'I don't mean that. I mean, that I'm here with someone I really like. It's the luxury of that I can't believe.'

Greg grunted softly.

He got the fire burning. The flames started off as tame little orange dancers, but eventually they bloomed into full, blood-red ones, that began to burn and crackle.

'There we are.'

'That's better,' Carol said.

Greg sat down – closer, almost beside her, and picked up his drink, taking another sip.

Carol stared into the fire, warmed by it. Mesmerised by the dancing flames. 'It's nice,' she said.

'Yes, it does change the atmosphere a little, doesn't it?' He looked up at the light. 'Hang on, I'll turn the light off and put the standard lamp on.'

'Greg, please, no,' Carol said, hastily grabbing his arm as he got up. 'Don't turn the light off.'

'The fire looks a little daft in the bright light, Carol,' he said, grinning. 'Trust me, it's okay.'

He went to turn the lamp on, which stood against the wall to the left of the room, near to the lounge door. It had a brass stand and a white shade with a faint floral pattern. He turned the overhead light off, putting the room in a relaxing, moody light.

'There, much better,' Greg said, and sat down again next to Carol on the sofa, with a slight gap in between them as before.

Carol sat there, quietly, unaware she was looking a bit depressed. She was looking down towards the floor and her eyes were open. She took a long, slow sip of her Martini again, and licked her lips, ignoring the tender soreness.

She was aware that Greg was still looking at her, but she continued to stare at the floor. It didn't bother her at all that Greg wanted to sit and look at her like that. The interest and attention was nice. It felt good. But the silence and this atmosphere put her in a reflective mood that made her think of things which she thought she had come here to escape from.

'If you want to talk about it, Carol, I'm more than happy to listen,' Greg said softly.

Carol grinned at him, appreciatively. 'There's not much to say about it really, is there? I married the wrong guy and I'm paying the price for it.'

'I don't think you should have to pay this much of a price, Carol.'

Carol shrugged. 'That's life, I suppose.'

Greg grunted. 'Well, I think you must have seen something special in him before, Carol, regardless of what he's like now,' he said. 'Like the animal magnetism you mentioned before.'

'Oh, yes. That was part of it, but it wasn't everything,' Carol said, looking directly at him. She took a deep breath, composed herself and looked downwards again. 'Before we were married, even for a short time after, Sean was just this wild, crazy, and exciting guy who made me enjoy life. He was strong too. Made me feel protected.' She said that with a disgustedly wry chuckle.

'We met in a pub one evening,' she continued. 'We had fun together. He made me laugh. And he excited me. So, not surprisingly, our sex life was wonderful as well. Always frisky and exciting. So, it wasn't long before we decided we were right for each other and... we were soon married.'

That's where Carol stopped.

'Go on, I'm listening,' Greg said.

'Are you sure you want to hear this?' she asked, looking at him doubtfully.

'Yes, I am sure. Go ahead, tell me,' Greg said, reassuringly.

She looked down again. 'Well at first, everything was okay, you know. I'd be waiting for him, when he came in from work, and he was always affectionate and playful. He always paid me attention. He'd squeeze my bum as he walked past me, grab me from behind. Things like that. And I admit, the vigorous sex-life we had together always turned me on. We had arguments, obviously.'

A very brief, hesitant pause. There was a lot of pain inside her trying to hide.

'But I soon noticed his temper. That scared me a bit. He lost it for silly reasons, the way it usually is. But it was more than that. His temper seemed so intense, it was more like a rage than a temper. And it wasn't long before the violence was directed towards me. I even remember the first time he actually hit me.

'We were in the kitchen, having an argument about something. Our voices were raised and it was getting a little heated up. Then, before I knew what was happening – out of nowhere, I was hit right across the face. I knew he'd just slapped me very hard, but it was the shock of it more than anything. I honestly didn't know what to think at the time. The slap was so vicious and there was no immediate apology or hint of regret in his face. He looked furious. I just looked at him, so hurt, and went up to the bedroom. Little did I know how bad things would get.'

'Did he ever apologise later for doing that?' Greg asked, his tone full of sympathy, not a hint of embarrassment in it at all.

Carol glanced at him. 'No. Not really,' she said. 'I don't think he ever apologised for the violence. He was angry, he hit me, that's all there was to it.' She paused a moment, reflectively. 'Of course, there were other things he did which were far worse.'

'My God,' Greg said with a light gasp, 'worse?'

'Yes. The jealous rages,' Carol said, with a tone ominous enough to startle Greg. Although, that wasn't her intention. The memory was just so awful.

'Jesus. What happened?'

She paused hesitantly again. She wasn't sure whether to cry or scream right now.

'We'd got home from a night out. This was the first time I remember it happening. A couple of guys at this club had started speaking to me. I talked to them and they asked about the bruise on my face. I told them I was attacked. They were actually convinced. Strange how you can convince two guys at a nightclub, but not a doctor at a hospital.'

'I think doctors know better,' Greg suggested.

'Do they?' Carol almost challenged. 'Pity they can't do anything about it.'

Greg sighed, maybe expressing some sympathy at the hopelessness of her situation. 'I'm sorry, I interrupted,' he said.

Carol glanced at him and continued. 'Well, I told them I was married, but I just spoke to them for a few minutes. They were friendly. They made me laugh as well. And they said I was cute, and I had nice hair. They soon went and left me alone, but, I don't know, Sean must have seen me speaking to them when he was getting drinks, he asked me who they were. I told him they were just talking to me. He looked suspicious, but I thought that was the end of it.

'But when we got in, his jealous rage exploded and he began firing questions and accusations at me. Why was I laughing with them? Why was I flirting? Why this? Why that? Then it got really nasty. He pushed me to the floor, said awful things… and that's when he… forced me, like a punishment.'

'Forced you? You mean…?'

Carol nodded. 'Raped me.'

Greg blew out a heavy sigh. He sounded shocked. But he didn't say anything.

Carol knew that something like that would be very hard for him to hear, but nowhere near as hard as it had been for her to tell him.

'I didn't think your own husband could do that. How stupid. He certainly made it feel like rape. The way he did it was creepy. The things he said. It felt like he was an outside attacker. It was frightening. It happened many times after that, so many that they all seem the same now, but it was always to hurt me however he could, to take sex from me rather than share it. Like a punishment. He liked doing it.'

She shuddered. Again, a pause.

'Anyway, the violence didn't stop. I tried to not make him lose his temper. But it hardly ever worked. The violence happened nearly all the time, every night.' Once more, she hesitated. 'Although, it wasn't always violence.'

She remembered that one night in particular when he could have killed her. And almost did. It wasn't a violent memory, but in many ways, it was worse. She couldn't help but think about it now. She had told Greg some truly awful things about the violence up to now, but she had left one of the worst things until last. This would probably shock him too.

'One night, he came up to me while I was in bed. I could feel him leaning over me. He started saying my name over and over. His voice was so calm, but it was also creepy. I opened my eyes and looked up at him. He was looking down on me with this strange, mean look in his eyes. I knew something was very wrong with him, and I dreaded to think what he was going to do.'

She hesitated again, sniffing. The terrible memories were overpowering her. She felt as if she might cry any minute. But she took a breath and gathered herself together to share with Greg one of the most frightening memories she could remember.

'He suddenly clamped my mouth shut with his hand, and he then brought his other hand down and pinched my nostrils together so I couldn't breathe. I stared up at him. He stared down at me, but he wouldn't let go. My hands were free and I did try to push him away and pull his hands off, but he was too strong. There was no way I could move them. Desperation almost made me feel strong enough, but I wasn't. I tried to breathe, I even tried to scream, but I couldn't. I prayed for him to let go, but I knew he wasn't going to. I panicked. I honestly thought he was going to kill me. My legs kicked, throwing the quilt off, my chest started to ache. I thought I was going to suffocate. But he finally let go. To this day, I don't even know why he did it. Maybe he just wanted to see what it was like to try and kill me, I don't know. Sometimes though, I honestly wished he'd have gone through with it.'

She was then silent, staring into the fire, unable to go into any more details. The memories were becoming too vivid now, too painful to recall. It also bothered her that she'd put up with it for so long, after telling him all this. She had told him more than enough.

Greg didn't say a word. Carol didn't expect him to. There was nothing much he could say that would make her feel any better.

She took a long gulp of her drink, nearly finishing it and then put her near-empty glass down beside the sofa and leaned her elbow on the sofa-arm. The lump in her throat became rock hard. Her eyes were ready to explode into tears. She covered them with her hand, sniffing even more, but she was already crying softly. She wanted to let it out.

'C-Carol?' was all Greg could manage in a choked-up whisper. He was obviously still shocked.

She felt his hand resting upon her shoulder gently, for reassurance, perhaps even for some kind of physical, understanding contact. Carol liked it. It wasn't too forward or presuming. It wasn't even intimate.

She turned towards him, leaned against him and wept into his chest, deliberately ignoring any discomfort she felt from the bruises on her body. He put his arm around her, squeezed gently, and just held her.

It was wonderfully warm and reassuring to be held in such a way. She enjoyed his arm around her and the cosiness of his chest. The fire warmed her too. And pretty soon, her weeping subsided, and she actually felt the pleasure of a grin creeping its way up her mouth.

Greg sat there in total disbelief after what Carol had just told him. It was shocking to think what she had been through. He knew domestic violence existed, he knew about the problem, but to have someone he cared about, a real-life sufferer actually talk to him about it, first hand in detail, had been extremely distressing, especially after having parents as happy as his had been.

It was strange, but he felt as if he should have been able to help her when he knew damned well he couldn't have done anything. He stared into the fire, enjoying Carol's soft and warm body in his arms.

Carol dozed and dozed peacefully, vaguely aware of her cosy and blissfully warm surroundings. She stirred a few times but did not wake. No one else woke her either. Her mind and body wanted to stay like this forever, cocooned in this time and place.

Time itself went on forever, and still she dozed, on the edge of deep sleep and of a peaceful dream.

Sean left the pub a little more than a couple of hours later in a much better mood. He'd had a few pints and something to eat and he'd had a good time with a couple of mates he knew in there. He'd also spoken to a nice young girl, who had seen his wedding ring, but hadn't minded speaking to him.

He wasn't in any real hurry to get home, but he felt better now than when he had come. He just hoped that Carol was not going to spoil his mood again when he got in. That would be just typical. And it would make him furious.

He passed a group of teenagers on the way back, laughing and chatting with each other and sharing cigarettes. He gave them a quick glance or two and continued on. They looked like trouble, huddled there together like that. But Sean was not the sort of bloke that they were going to pick a fight with.

He walked on, totally unaware that Carol was not going to be waiting for him when he got in.

It was Greg who first managed to open his eyes wide enough to realise that they were still sitting in the same place in front of the fire and that time had not come to a temporary standstill.

He had never expected to doze off like that. He would've stayed like that forever if it was possible. So would Carol probably.

He looked down at Carol. She was still leaned against his chest, dozing. It was certainly a heavy doze. She might even have been fast asleep. He grinned and looked forward. The fire burned on. He looked to his right and instinctively up at the wall clock.

The time practically stared down at him. The look on his face turned into panic. His eyes widened. He couldn't believe it.

My God, it can't be, he thought. But it was. And he dreaded telling Carol.

*

Carol was still dozing against his chest, on the edge of deep sleep and having a peaceful dream about meeting Greg earlier that afternoon, when all of a sudden, her peaceful slumber was interrupted by Greg's voice, which had an edge of importance to it that brought her back to reality a little quicker.

'Carol,' he said. 'Hey, Carol, wake up.'

She pulled up from him, slowly, sighed sleepily and blinked several times, then rubbed her eyes a little. 'Wow,' she said. 'I must have dozed off.'

'Yes, actually we both did,' Greg said.

Carol looked at him and saw the expression on his face.

'Greg, what's wrong?' she asked.

'I'm sorry, Carol,' Greg said, 'but I'm afraid we've let time slip us by a little.'

Carol frowned at him. 'What?'

Greg looked at her, then pointed at the clock on the wall up to his right.

Carol looked up at it and suddenly panicked. Her eyes widened in disbelief.

'*Nooo*! No, it can't be!'

Greg leaned back on the sofa, and threw his arms up behind his head, obviously sickened by what he had just done.

'I'm sorry,' he said. 'That was selfish of me. I should've—'

'No, it's my fault!' Carol almost squealed. 'Jesus, Greg, we've gotta go! We've got to get back before Sean does!'

Her world was suddenly thrown into complete chaos. She was in a blind panic. Her mind raced, her thoughts jammed, crashing into irrationality. She couldn't think straight.

What the hell had she been thinking, dozing off like that, as if there were no consequences to her actions? What did she think this was, some romantic night for two? She had to get back into the real world.

Sean would be back any minute now. He was going to kill her! What had she done? How could she have been so stupid?

She got up, raced to the lounge door, realised she'd forgotten her handbag, went back for it and raced to the door again.

Greg didn't budge.

'Greg! Please, come *on*!' Carol pleaded. She couldn't understand why he was still sitting there, as if nothing was wrong.

'Carol, even if we left now, there's no guarantee we'd be back before Sean. He's probably home already,' he said.

Carol just looked at him. She couldn't believe this.

'Anyway, what could you possibly say to him if you did go back at this time of night?'

Time still moved on. The clock ticked to 11.22.

'My God,' Carol said, breathing nervously, her hand up against her face. 'What am I going to do? He's going to kill me.' She couldn't get her terrified voice much higher than a whisper. 'He's really going to kill me. How could I have been so stupid? What am I going to do?'

She stood there, feeling lost, vulnerable and afraid, and for one terrible moment, she thought she was going to collapse right there under the strain and humiliate herself in front of Greg.

Greg, quite hastily, got to his feet and stood there, looking in Carol's direction. 'Carol, wait a minute,' he said.

'But, Greg, what am I gonna do?' she said, in tears again. 'He's going to kill me!'

'Carol,' Greg said, more firmly, and a little impatient, it seemed. 'Listen to me. He's not going to kill you – at least not tonight.'

Carol looked at him with a frown, completely thrown, as Greg approached her, slowly.

What did he mean by that?

'Deep down – I don't think you had any intention of going home tonight at all. If you had, then you would've kept an eye on the time like a hawk. But you didn't. You couldn't have cared less about the time. I think you were too busy enjoying yourself.'

Whatever gave him that idea? she wondered.

'That's not true,' Carol said, without much conviction.

'Sorry, Carol, I think it is.' He had now walked right up to her. Close enough to hold her. 'You came here this evening because you wanted to. You stayed a long time because you wanted to. You knew that if you stayed for long enough, then it wouldn't matter about the time. You wanted to be with me just as I wanted to be with you.'

Carol was shaking her head, weakly, but deep inside, she had doubts. Was Greg right? Had she really done that? Somehow, she couldn't believe she had. Well, whether she had or not, Carol felt what little defences she had, weakening rapidly. And once again, with Greg so close to her, both psychologically and physically, her heart-rate began to respond.

'No, no,' Carol said weakly, almost in denial of what her heart-rate was telling her, 'that's not—'

'Deep down, you're sick and tired of the violence and abuse from Sean,' Greg said, not letting her finish, but he spoke gently, 'there was nothing you could do to stop it, so when the chance came, you finally decided to have some respect for yourself. You decided to turn your back on the violence, which you wanted to do and be with someone who you wanted to be with, someone who would treat you with the care and respect that, deep down, you know you deserve.'

'Noo, nooo,' Carol said, now in tears, her defences collapsing, falling apart around her. She had turned away from Greg and had grabbed the lounge door handle, but she was making no attempt at all to open it. She simply held onto it for dear life, mainly to stop herself from collapsing right there in front of him.

'For the first time in your life, you made a decision which made you feel good about yourself. For a change, you put Sean right out of your mind, and thought about your own feelings, and you were able to really relax and let yourself go, to feel the pleasure, and I think you enjoyed it.'

'Noooo, nooooo—'

'You didn't really care about the time did you? You had no intention of going back tonight,' Greg said, sounding as if he respected Carol a great deal for acting so bravely.

'No,' Carol said, mostly to herself, not in answer to Greg's question, but it was so weak, it was barely audible. Her head had stopped shaking and she simply wept it out, gently.

'That is the truth, isn't it, Carol?' he asked gently.

Carol was still turned away from him, looking down at the handle.

Where the hell had all that come from? Carol couldn't help but wonder. It was as if he'd reached right down into her very soul and had pulled it free. It was flying right now. But it was so high, she had no idea of where it was going. She also felt slightly dizzy.

'Isn't it?'

Carol slowly looked back up at him. She let go of the handle and dropped her handbag to the floor. Completely resigned.

'What the hell am I going to do?' she asked him. 'I'm scared, Greg, I'm so scared. Everything has just become such a mess.'

'I don't think so,' Greg said. 'I'm glad things worked out like this. I'm in love with you.'

Carol blinked in amazement. *Well, where the hell had* that *come from*? she thought to herself. But she couldn't deny it, it excited her that he felt that way. The question was, did she feel the same way about him? She shouldn't have had to ask herself that, but she did.

'You've only known me for barely a day. How could you possibly be in love with me?'

'Easily,' Greg replied, grinning proudly. 'Believe me.'

Carol sniffed, then grinned back. Her lips quivered slightly.

'It's still a mess,' she said. 'Sean.'

Greg sighed, as if he was tired of hearing Sean's name. But Carol knew he was also afraid. If not more so. Carol had lived with him. Greg had never even met him. And from what she had told him up to now, Carol knew that Greg had good reason to be scared.

'Maybe,' he said. 'But as I said, it's no use worrying about him now. He's probably home already, and even if he's not, he'll be there before we are. We'll worry about him later. There's no point in worrying about it now. Let's just put the time we have together now to good use.'

Carol felt her heart flutter.

Her grin widened. 'And how do you suggest we do that?'

But Carol knew perfectly well.

Greg looked deeply into her eyes, something which made Carol swallow. She was drawn in again. She was allowing herself to be drawn in. Her hand was leaning against the wall, next to the lounge door and her knee was slightly bent forward. She began to shiver, even though the room was warm with the fire. Her heart thumped. She had the strongest feeling that he was about to kiss her. But she didn't move. She simply waited.

'Sorry, Carol,' Greg said, softly, still looking deeply into her eyes, 'but I can't hold this back any longer. I'm not even sure that I want to.'

Carol stood there, rooted to the spot, her own eyes not moving at all away from his. She revelled in his deep gaze as his mouth approached hers, it made her heart gallop all the more faster.

Oh my God, she suddenly thought, *this is really happening*.

She was really going to do this.

★

Carol couldn't remember the last time she'd felt this excited. Everything had more or less come down to this moment. It was the moment of truth for both of them. It was a terrifying and exciting moment that they had both waited very patiently for. And rightly so. They had no guarantees that it would work between them, but this was the right time to find out, no question about it. The wait was paying off.

Greg's mouth was slightly open as he bent down to kiss her, and he had to go quite a way, as he was a good eight inches or so taller than her – which he did teasingly slowly, almost treating her like a schoolgirl waiting for her first real kiss. And it did wonders to turn Carol on. Her heart accelerated harder, faster, as Greg came in closer. Her head almost spun, and her stomach was in a pleasant whirl. She felt weak at the knees.

As he came within an inch or two of her mouth, she didn't know whether to pull back or not, the frightened part of her almost wanted to, but she didn't, instead, she naturally closed her eyes, and pulled back only slightly, tightening her neck muscles, just seconds before their lips touched.

As soon as they did touch, Carol's heart leapt. She hauled in a deep breath, her chest rose up, her breasts swelled, reached out and her nipples hardened against her blouse. And to Carol, after so much suffering, it felt fantastic. It also felt irresistible. She couldn't believe it, but she loved it. And, once again, she didn't even think about the bruising around her mouth.

He kissed her softly to begin with, and Carol stood there enjoying it, but she also responded, kissing him softly, slowly, making drawn out sighs and moans. Their lips made soft sounds, and Carol could have gone on like this forever. Her mind, her soul was floating, free. As free as it had ever been, and her excitement remained high, taking her to places she never would have imagined. The bruises didn't exist.

Greg then suddenly stopped and drew back, licking his lips. He was grinning, and looking quite breath-taken.

Carol looked up at him not knowing what to say.

She wondered why he had stopped.

They were still looking at each other; a strange, somewhat hesitant, unsure gaze passing between them. But neither of them said anything.

Carol blinked a few times, uncertain of what Greg was thinking. She was still wondering why he had stopped. He didn't have doubts did he? Carol didn't believe so. Maybe he was just testing the moment, wondering if it was going in the right direction; wondering if Carol wanted to carry on and also wondering if she'd liked the kiss.

She had. For heaven's sake, she had. She was begging him inside to kiss her again.

All she could do was stare up at him, waiting, trying to breathe calmly, with her heartbeat still keeping up its galloping pace. It hadn't slowed down much at all. Actually, this hesitation was also exciting her, turning her on. Did he know that?

Greg gazed down at her, still with a grin on his face. A grin Carol returned. The silence continued. Neither of them said anything. But they didn't have to. It was the way Greg looked at her that said it all. She looked back at him in the same way. The kiss was fantastic. It had told both her and Greg all they needed to know.

In the background, the fire was steadily losing life, but they were not really interested in the fire at the moment.

It had seemed an eternity since Carol had felt this good. The excitement and deep emotion Carol felt now, left her totally lost in all this. And it was wonderful.

It was wonderful to be able to feel lost again, to be able to let herself be free, without fear of consequence, without fear of any kind, even though the fear was playing some small part in freeing her now, hidden away in some shadowy corner where it lay in wait.

Her hand dropped away from the wall beside the door, hanging hesitantly by her side, her knee straightened out and she took a tiny step towards him and stood upright.

Carol's eyes were almost demanding that Greg kiss her again. She stood there waiting, not saying a word.

Greg's grin widened, as he bent down to kiss her again.

Carol responded, her hand reaching out to his waist.

As he kissed her again, Carol's response was strong and immediate.

The last few moments alone had seemed like forever, and even though they hadn't known each other for very long, it seemed like they had. There was something special between them and right now, Carol responded.

Their kiss went on. A little firmer than before, sucking gently at each other's lips, and impulsively, Carol's hand moved across his waist, up towards his chest, followed by her other hand and then they slipped right up towards his neck, lifting her closer towards him.

She could feel Greg's hands too, moving around her waist, enjoying her soft curves, and that's when her arms moved up and wrapped slowly, but firmly around Greg's neck, lifting her up even closer towards him, so that her heels raised slightly off the floor. She made another drawn out sigh of pleasure.

Carol knew that she'd crossed the point of no return and her body was responding in a way she never thought possible, but she allowed herself to enjoy it.

His hands ran gently up and down Carol's back as they kissed. The warmth and tenderness that ran through them as he glided them up and down, was wonderful. The feeling of being cuddled and caressed in such a way. It pushed and grinded her up against him more and more and made her moan with pleasure. And naturally, of course, they pulled each other in very close now. Carol's cleavage was up against Greg's chest. Her legs were pinned together, and her buttocks were deliciously clenched. Her arms tightened around Greg's neck and Greg's arms wrapped more firmly around Carol's body, tightening around her and pushing her breasts even more firmly against him.

Their kissing became firmer, more intense, as Carol grew hungrier, gently exploring Greg's mouth with her tongue. The bruise beside Carol's mouth was now gone, to another darker time and place, as it did nothing to stop her from enjoying this satisfying and rather important moment. It was too good.

Greg was obviously getting hungrier too, as he pulled her in continuously, as if he couldn't hold her close enough and Carol didn't resist in the slightest, and his hand then slid down her back to her skirt and rested on her bottom, unable to resist squeezing gently. Another exciting moment for Carol, which again made her sigh heavily, as it was the first sexually intimate thing he'd done since they'd met.

Then, to Carol's pleasant surprise, Greg pulled away from her and began to kiss the side of her face, around the side of her neck and around her ear, tickling her with his tongue and nibbling her ear-lobe. Greg was obviously getting more confident and ambitious now after the bravely intimate move of reaching down to put his hand on her bottom. Carol's nose twitched, cutely. She smiled broadly and emitted a sharp, throaty giggle, which inspired Greg to continue the quest. Sharp, sizzling sensations raced through Carol like wildfire. Her body shuddered excitedly. She made groaning noises and her hand clutched eagerly at Greg's neck.

Carol couldn't help it. The pleasure was undeniable, irresistible. She wanted more.

Greg couldn't believe this.

He had sensed a passion in Carol, but he'd had no idea it was as strong or as wonderful as this. This woman was bringing something out in him that he never even knew he had.

And all that he'd said to her a few moments ago, about why she had stayed, where on earth had all that come from?

No matter. They had all night. This was worth waiting for. He didn't want the quest to end here though, the fire was much warmer.

*

Carol was making near-purring noises as she clutched at Greg's neck and enjoyed his lips against the now goose-pimpled flesh of her neck. Her lips quivered and she almost hung against him.

Greg then whispered into her ear; 'Weren't we sitting by a nice, warm fire not a few moments ago?'

'I don't mind standing here,' she gasped back.

'Still, it would be nice, wouldn't it?' Greg whispered into her ear again.

She reluctantly pulled away and looked at him, her hands sliding back down his chest to his waist.

She turned and looked at the weakening flames. Then, she turned back to look at Greg.

For a moment, she was undecided. She honestly thought they would have been ready to make love by now, but the time seemed oddly not quite right. After all, they did have all night. So there was no hurry at all. She had no reason to hurry.

Greg's grin was a curious one.

His curiosity was arousing. Carol knew that she had the freedom now and could do anything she wanted. But nothing too extravagant. There was plenty of time. Simplicity was the best thing here. Simple, but provocative, and in the smallest way possible.

Take something off.

She pulled her hands back from his waist, grinned into his eyes and then slowly took off her shoes. They were strapless slip-ons, so they were easy to remove. But that alone felt like she was taking off much more. She then reached up under her skirt and rolled down her stockings, something she didn't expect to do, but she did it without thinking and by instinct, enjoying the smooth skin of her own thighs and calves. It was a nice sensation which made her blush; the forbidden nature of enjoying her own body.

She stood there with the pleasing sensation of the soft carpet against her bare feet. She stood there with her toes curling up, her legs pinned together again, now feeling even better now they were bare, and her hands resting against his chest again, grinning at him, unsure what to feel right now. But whatever it was, she knew there was room for more and that there was better to come.

She then turned and walked barefoot, back towards the fire, and curled up on the floor in front of it. She looked around at Greg, waiting for him.

Greg grinned back, liking the idea, and took off his shoes. He too came back to the fire, Carol's eyes following him all the way. He revamped the fire, until the flames were brought to life again – a few grinning glances at Carol as he did so, and then he sat down behind her on the floor, legs stretched out beside her, and put his arms around her shoulders.

Carol looked at the flames, and leaned back against him, enjoying the warmth. Greg tightened his arms firmly around her shoulders and chest, and squeezed lovingly. With one hand, he then brushed her hair behind her ear, she felt his fingers run gently through the silky strands, which made Carol purr luxuriously and tilt her head. He kissed her ear and held her again. Carol leaned her head right back against him, relaxed and closed her eyes.

She could still see Greg's face in the darkness.

Sean was in a very ugly rage.

What looked like a million pieces of broken crockery were scattered across the kitchen floor, after Sean had smashed plates and saucers and cups down. He had upturned the dining table chairs and he had been kicking and punching everything in sight; doors, cupboards, chairs. He'd kicked at the broken crockery on the floor. He had roared abuse at the top of his voice, which was intended for Carol, but she wasn't here, so it'd simply poisoned the air, but he was definitely going to teach her a lesson when she came back.

But the shock of coming home to an empty house! Jesus! He couldn't *believe* it. His mind had exploded with anger and humiliation. After all they had been through. Where the hell had that bitch disappeared to? How dare she run off like this?

Sean was now roaming up and down the hall, working off his rage, going in and out of the kitchen, the lounge, unable to stay in one place for very long. He was perspiring heavily, furious with Carol for doing this to him. Not just for leaving him alone, but for making him so mad. The rage was building up inside him again, consuming him, like a savage, crazy hunger, fuelled by hate, like coals being shovelled relentlessly into the hot, grinding energy of a steam train's engine, and there was no way to stop it, no release.

But why stop it anyway? Was it really so bad? He felt like a machine, an engine, a powerful engine, driven on by madness; out of control, and loving it. He felt invincible.

He continued his rampage through the house, his rage all consuming; thinking about her, thinking about what she had done, thinking about where she was and what she was doing now, although Sean knew, or suspected anyway.

Instinctively, he knew the only thing she could be doing. She had nowhere else to go.

She was with someone. She was with another bloke. That bitch was with another bloke. That had to be it. He was sure of it. He may not know who he was, but Sean could just imagine the two of them in bed, sleeping together. Laughing at him. Thinking they could get away with it. It made his blood boil, and his rage stronger.

Well, he would teach her. There was no way she was going to screw some other bloke and get away with it. He was going to make her pay. Maybe even him too. Whoever he was.

Well, Sean didn't care who he was, there was no way she was going to stay with him. She would have to come back. He knew she would come back. Or she would be in serious trouble. He would make sure of it.

'Oh, yes,' Sean said to himself, 'I'll get you for this. I know you'll come back. And when you do, I'm gonna make you pay for this. I'll be waiting.' And he would wait. It was only a matter of time before she returned. She would have to return. He knew she would. And when she returned, he would be ready for her, no matter what.

He then went to the kitchen, looked down, saw the mess of crockery on the floor, and he gave it an almighty kick.

Carol felt as if she was going to melt and float away. Her body wasn't used to feeling such intense pleasure. It felt strange. It'd been so long since she had felt pleasure or excitement of any kind, that she had practically forgotten what it was like to feel good at all. She was full of sighs and giggles.

She was also well aware of how scared she was. But the fear was a combination of so many things; where she was, what she was doing, what would happen if this night ever reached the point of no return, how she would cope if she would never be able to see Greg again with the love she felt for him now.

This was the amazing thing. These feelings of glorious pleasure did not go away, they made her drift, but she hadn't dozed off again, she was very much awake and very much aware of the problems she had now. She was scared, more than she could say, but that wasn't stopping her from feeling the love she had for Greg. She could admit it at last. But could she say it to him?

In some shadowy corner of her mind, she also couldn't help but think of what she had done. Thinking about Sean in the house alone, wondering where she was.

What he must have done when he found out she was gone. The images were dark and haunting. She could picture him, in his rage, prowling the streets like a wild animal, hunting for her, searching in every house – coming to get her.

She took a deep breath. She couldn't think about it.

He was still there and it would have to be dealt with.

But if she was to enjoy this night, make the most of it, while believing that this could be her only chance to be with Greg, then it was time for her to let go and not be afraid just for now. To hell with the consequences. The reality at the moment was too special to ruin with fear.

'You know, I still can't believe I'm really here,' Carol said suddenly, without really thinking about it.

'I told you, Carol, you're here because you want to be. You're enjoying yourself. Anyway, I thought we'd been through all that,' he said.

'I know,' Carol said, relaxed against Greg's chest. 'I just find it incredible to believe that I'm actually here, knowing in the back of my mind what Sean's going to do. I bet he's going out of his mind at home at the moment.'

Greg chuckled wryly behind her. 'Well, I bet he's not going out of his mind with worry,' he said. 'Jealousy perhaps. And frustration, because he can't hit you.'

'Maybe so,' Carol said. 'But you must understand, Greg, underneath all the violence and abuse, there's a man I once loved. He used to make me feel good.'

Carol didn't know why she was defending Sean, but right now, she still felt a need to.

'I do understand that, Carol,' Greg said. 'But there's something I think you must understand too. I mean, I know I don't know him, but from what you've told me, the man you say you once loved… well, he's changed, I mean, he… well he certainly isn't the man you married, that's for sure.'

Carol said nothing.

She didn't particularly want to go into this subject right now, even though she had brought it up. She'd only just managed to put it out of her mind.

Greg obviously thought the same.

'Let's drop this subject, Carol. Let's not spoil the mood, eh?' he said.

Carol still said nothing.

Greg then said; 'I would like you to know, however, that I'm in love with you.'

It was the second time that Greg had said it to her and she knew she should take it seriously because there was no doubt that he meant it. But also, Carol knew she felt the same about him, even in only a short time. But would she be able to tell him? Greg would certainly hope so.

Well, there was no harm in admitting it, it was obvious to both of them anyway. It was time to say so.

'Oh, God help me,' Carol said. 'I think I'm in love with you too.'

'Phew! Thank Christ for that,' Greg said wryly, but she could tell he was relieved that she had said it. To be honest, so was she.

He was holding her around the chest, rather loosely. It was somehow better this way to enjoy the softness and the comfort of being held. He sent pleasant shivers down her spine as he planted warm, affectionate kisses on the back of her neck, pushing her beautiful auburn hair out of the way. Beautiful as it was, in this mixture of dancing firelight and the soft, moody glow of the standard lamp behind them to their left, it had taken on a spectacular, fiery life of its own. Carol couldn't see it yet for herself, but she knew. It almost felt as if it'd been given a new life and the chance to shine with the energy she knew it had.

The kisses sent shivers down her spine. The fire burned brightly. It warmed her. Its peaceful, friendly crackling and Greg's warm hands relaxed her.

Carol's breathing was steady, but rather deep. Her mouth was slightly open and the corners were turned up into a grin. Her eyes were closed, and her head was still leaning back against Greg's chest.

Carol heard him whisper something into her ear; she didn't hear it properly, but she didn't ask him to repeat it either.

This was really the point of no return.

It was the moment they had been building up to all night. Especially the past hour or so, since their first kiss. Carol just knew somehow that it was about to happen.

It was unnerving, it was strange, it was exhilarating, it was so relaxing.

Greg's hands moved down to her bust, held her breasts, and gently squeezed them through her jumper. Carol's breath jumped. Her eyes flickered open and shut. She knew what Greg was doing, but she didn't utter a word of objection. The corners of her mouth straightened out, wondering what he was going to do next. Her eyes roved from side to side. Her heart began to thud.

His hands moved slowly down over her bust, then down to her stomach. The slow movement of his hands was nervous, almost hesitant, but his hands were flat down against her stomach and they were always moving. She didn't feel them stop at any time. And they moved up and down a lot, up and down, more and more, as if they were eager to do something, to go somewhere. They moved down, then up again, but Carol got the sense that she knew that it was down, down that they wanted to go. Moving back up was the hesitation, the nervousness. They wanted to go down, perhaps so that his fingertips could slide down into her skirt. She almost gave him a helping hand and pushed them down. But she didn't. It was up to him. She had to let him do it naturally.

Her heart banged excitedly against her chest, pumping the

blood and adrenaline through her body, and she was sure that Greg's heart was hammering against her back, one heartbeat directly behind the other.

Suddenly, she felt his hands try to slide down into her skirt, but maybe there was nowhere else for them to go, as he pulled them up again and got a hold of Carol's jumper instead and the blouse she wore under it, and he slowly pulled them up, still kissing Carol's neck and ear, possibly trying to cover up and hide what he was doing with his hands.

Carol could feel the blouse moving against her skin, sliding seductively up her waist, creeping teasingly out of her skirt. Greg had already pulled them up far enough to expose the first glimpse of her soft, flat stomach to the moody, quiet world of the lounge. The few marks on it were invisible. There was no pain in here. Carol didn't even think about him seeing them.

It was the second time tonight that Carol had felt exposed, naked in some way (the other time being when she had taken off her shoes).

It was only her stomach, but somehow it felt like she was revealing so much more. The thrill of showing off her smooth flesh to him was becoming even more exciting. Knowing Greg felt strongly for her, gave her the confidence to enjoy everything that he saw, and felt, for herself.

Carol put her hands on Greg's hands as he pulled her jumper and blouse up, but she made no attempt to stop him.

'Greg—' Carol said in hardly a whisper, but she said no more.

Greg put his hands flat onto her stomach and Carol smiled with pleasure as she heard his gasp of delight in her ear. He was really enjoying this as well. Good.

Her blouse was now pulled all the way out of her skirt and both that and her jumper hung loosely on Greg's arms as they wrapped around Carol's naked waist.

Carol's breathing remained steady, but deep. The further this went, the more emotional and sexually aware she became. It was like surrendering to the forbidden. Her mind was jammed with torrents of pleasure. Lost in a world she hadn't known for a long time.

All of a sudden, Greg turned her towards him, leaning her back and cradling her with his arms. Her legs straightened out in front of her. It was a move that took Carol by surprise and she looked up at him rather intensely. He looked afraid. Maybe he didn't know what else to do. Carol didn't care. She was full of wonder, trying to anticipate what he was going to do next.

As Greg came down to kiss her again, her heart galloped. He kissed her and there was something different about the kiss this time. It was a lot deeper, more passionate than before. There was much more of a hunger there.

Carol's arm impulsively went around Greg's neck again. She moved in close and her other hand slipped out and then went to pull Greg's shirt out of his trousers – which she did, and for a moment, her hands were on his waist, and then moving all over his back, enjoying his soft skin, and that's when she found herself pulling him down, with Greg more than happy to do what she wanted.

Before Carol knew it, she was lying flat on the floor – sofa almost right next to them, her legs stretched out in front of her and Greg right above her. She could feel his body weight up against her side.

Carol raised her knee and ran her bare leg along Greg's legs, enjoying the soft material of his trousers against the sensitive inside of her thigh.

His hand became adventurous as they kissed – long, lingering, soft kisses that made Carol smile, his hand stroked and caressed her stomach, floating up and down it, like a boat on a gentle sea. He caressed her side, and moved up and across under her blouse.

His hand was heading for her bra.

Greg must have realised this and didn't want to rush anything, as he pulled his hand away and she suddenly felt it on her thigh, gliding up and down it as she ran her leg up against his.

He was kissing her around the neck and ear now. Her hand was all over him too. She had pulled his shirt out of his trousers and was now caressing his back and sides.

Greg's hand came further down the back of her thigh, making her leg pull up closer and making her abdomen tighten. His hand then slipped right up into her skirt, which Carol knew had more or less pulled right up as she could feel the fire's warmth directly on her upper thighs, and he touched the soft material of her knickers. He even had the courage to slip his fingers under her knickers and feel the soft, fleshy skin of her buttock.

Having such an arousing part of her body touched made Carol moan in delight and it also made her even hungrier. Her hand moved down to his bottom and she started to squeeze. But squeezing his bum through his trousers – nice though it was, wasn't satisfying enough. She was hungry for more.

Carol then slipped her hand around to the front of Greg's trousers and took a hold of him.

Greg suddenly grunted in surprise and Carol felt his hand, still inside her knickers stroking her buttock, moving around to the front of her knickers, where he touched her between the legs.

Greg suddenly stopped as soon as he touched her there, and Carol opened her eyes. He breathed deeply into her face, sounding afraid, but also excited.

'I'm sorry,' he whispered. 'I just can't believe how fast this is going.'

'It's okay. I like it. I'm enjoying it,' Carol whispered back up to him. 'It feels good.'

'I'm sorry, I seem to have spoilt the mood a bit,' he said, embarrassed.

Carol just grinned, looking directly up at him.

She sat up again, glancing around at him and running her hand along his thigh. She met his eyes again with another grin and then got to her feet, smoothing down her skirt.

Carol took a couple of steps towards the window, her arms folded. She imagined that Greg thought she was disappointed, when in fact nothing could be further from the truth, she was delighted. She felt wonderful.

'I'm sorry,' Greg said behind her. 'I've ruined it haven't I?'

Carol smiled to herself. Greg couldn't see. 'Are you a virgin, Greg?'

She heard him grunt. Possibly surprised by such a frank question.

'Sorry?'

'I asked if you were a virgin,' she said gently.

'Yes. And I'm not ashamed of it either. I nearly lost my virginity when I was eighteen, but I didn't feel ready. Why do you ask?'

Carol knew he was somehow. Which made this feel even

better. She turned around to face him, smiling.

Greg was amazed. He thought she was disappointed.

She enjoyed his surprise.

Greg smiled back and got to his feet.

'Because I believe everybody's first time should be extra special,' she said, gazing up at him.

She grabbed the bottom of her beige jumper, pulled it up over her head, off her arms and tossed it aside, shaking and smoothing her auburn hair back into shape, and pushing it behind her ears again.

She took a couple of steps towards him, her heart hammering against her chest, as she slowly undid the buttons on her blouse, right down to the last one, grinning provocatively up into Greg's eyes, as she pulled it completely free of her skirt, and slipped it off, exposing a white nylon bra, what Greg had been close to touching about five minutes ago.

Greg gazed down at her, looking awe-struck.

She took a step closer and undid some of the buttons on his shirt. She then moved in, closed her eyes and kissed his chest.

She undid more buttons, while kissing, sucking and biting him and she felt Greg remove his shirt and she kissed him all over. She kissed his chest, kissed and sucked at his nipples and then his chest again, while she felt Greg's fingers lightly stroking up and down her arms and her hair, which felt so glorious.

Carol kissed him lower down, and then got down on her knees and kissed his stomach. She kissed, sucked and licked his stomach, eyes closed, loving every inch of his skin, and that's when she started to undo the front of his trousers.

Carol listened to Greg's gasps and nervous breathing above, and she stopped and gazed up at him.

His expression was full of wonder, and he was grinning down at her. He looked afraid, but he wasn't objecting to anything, and it looked as if there was so much that he wanted to say, and all of it was good.

Carol smiled up at him and continued.

Greg was right about one thing – this was going fast, and up to now, the night still seemed to be lasting forever, even though it was still quite early.

She undid the button and hook on his trousers and then pulled his zip down, loosening them.

Now it was Carol's turn to feel nervous and a little awe-struck.

When she pulled his trousers down past his hips, she couldn't help but gasp with delight and be filled with pride when she saw how much he'd grown in front. It was almost larger than life itself, sticking right out towards her and almost coming out of his white briefs.

She gazed up at him again, thought what the hell, and decided to just go for it. Her heart was hammering so hard, she almost couldn't control her breathing. She grabbed his briefs, tugged hard at the elastic and pulled them down with his trousers.

The sudden whip of elastic down his legs was a wonderfully sexy and predatory sound and Carol had managed to bring his briefs right down to his knees. They looked as if they had just happily obeyed a command. His erection bobbed up and down a little before becoming still again and Carol gazed at it, happily.

Greg made a heavy grunt of amazement above her.

Carol didn't give him oral though. Not now. She gently licked it up and down with the tip of her tongue, smiling as she did so and stroking his buttocks, and then she gently kissed the tip of it.

She got up on her feet again and just stood there looking at him.

They were both perspiring lightly. A pleasant scent hung in the air. It wasn't hot though. The fire warmed what was otherwise a cool night. There was a thrilling sense of anticipation of what was to come. And the firelight danced on their bodies, as if daring them.

Carol didn't think her heart could thump any harder, but it did. Surely Greg could see it hammering inside her chest. She glanced down, then up at him again, and waited.

Greg grinned and took his trousers off, then his socks and then his briefs. He was blushing still, but he didn't seem embarrassed, as he stood there naked in front of her.

Carol was nowhere near naked yet. She was enjoying teasing him. She liked his body too. His slim and lightly-hairy chest and legs. He looked so wonderfully smooth.

She gazed up at him, while raising her hands, slowly, and

slipped the straps of her bra off her shoulders and slowly reached up behind to unclip it.

Carol's adrenaline pumped through her as if her life depended on it. She was almost afraid that her bra was holding her heart in as well as her breasts, and if she took it off, her heart would pop out. It felt incredible.

She unhooked her bra, and her grin widened even more, as she let the cups slip right off her breasts and be cradled in her arms, then she dropped it to the floor and stood there smiling, glowing with life, with her arms by her sides, pushing her chest out, proudly, her delight swelling, as Greg looked at her breasts with admiration. They were a nice size, well-shaped, and they hung nicely, and were soft-looking with dark pink nipples. Carol obviously knew what her own breasts looked like, but to her they always seemed unremarkable. Ordinary. Nothing to boast about. But not now. Now they were exciting, beautiful, seductive and alluring. And right now, Carol felt their incredibly alluring sexual power more than ever. Her smile glowed more than her delight.

She then reached back and undid the back of her skirt – while Greg watched eagerly, as she fiddled it around her hips to loosen it and allowed it to slip down her legs and drop freely to the floor around her feet. It felt delicious. Wonderfully exposing. She felt so free. And sexy. She stepped out of the skirt and kicked it aside, and stood there in her briefs.

They moved into each other again and kissed and Carol felt safe and snug pressed up against Greg's nakedness. Especially her warm breasts squashed lightly up against his chest. The first real contact they'd had.

She then felt Greg try to slip his hands down into her knickers, but she grabbed his hands, stopped him and pulled back.

She stood there smiling. Greg looked worried.

'You'll be getting plenty of that upstairs,' she whispered to him.

Greg just smiled again.

'Where's your bedroom?'

'First on the right,' Greg whispered back.

Carol glanced down, took his hand and then slowly walked past him. She looked back at him again with a grin that didn't know whether to be provocative, tantalising or inviting.

Carol thought she saw a flash of trepidation in his eyes, but Greg walked with her, as she led him out of the lounge and took him upstairs to his own bedroom.

Carol knew that Greg was looking at her buttocks moving beneath her knickers, as he followed naked behind her, as she had glanced around and caught him at it twice, and she could feel it, but she was hoping he was. This game of teasing was so much fun. But the teasing would be over soon.

There were other wonderful things that awaited discovery, and the idea of going up to Greg's bedroom to continue the journey, where she would gladly give Greg everything, (with her knickers on, she wasn't even nude yet), including the softness between her legs, which right now felt very wet and eager, filled Carol with an even more powerful sense of excitement and limitless possibilities.

This night was far from over.

*

Greg's bedroom. Moonlit shadows coming in from the window between open curtains, filling nearly every corner.

Carol standing by the bed, with Greg behind her, bending over in front of him, and pulling her knickers down her soft rump and legs, delighting in the feeling of finally being naked in front of him and showing off her bottom, before standing up straight and crawling seductively into Greg's bed, like a sexy feline claiming its new found territory, and finally slipping in, luxuriating and purring endlessly at the cosy warmth and comfort that surrounded her. His bed, (another man's bed), was wonderful. It was like a sea of tranquillity, a cloud riding higher than her very soul was right now. And again, it made Carol feel as if she were floating. There was an atmosphere of peace, almost heaven-like, in the velvety, moon-shadowed darkness.

Then Greg was on top of her, more or less; she could feel his weight climbing into bed next to her and she saw him, his large figure cloaked in velvety shadows, moving in next to her. And she immediately wrapped her arms around him, welcoming his body warmth.

He kissed her right on her mouth, on the corners, above and below her lips, then her cheeks. His hands caressed her side and stroked her hair. She couldn't help but smile as he kissed her, thinking about how far she had come and how far this could go. Their enjoyment was the same, even though they had come so far already. It was wonderful to be naked with him. But there was still so much left, and while cloaked in this wonderful, moonlit darkness, on this endless night in which the possibilities were as exciting as they were infinite, Carol couldn't help but lose herself in the fantasy of it, making the most of what she secretly feared may be only the one night she'd have with him.

She pulled him in closer so he was on top of her. He kissed her mouth again and her face and he kissed her neck and nibbled around her ear. She shivered deliciously against him, sucking air through her teeth, hungry for more. Her hands ran up and down the smooth plain of his back, loving the contours of his shoulder blades and the ridge of his spine. She loved the way her breasts were squashed against her under the weight of his chest, with her hard, swelling nipples having nowhere to hide. She had an insatiable urge to melt right into him, to become a part of him and leave this world behind forever.

He then moved down and kissed her neck again, right on the tender side, and she felt his mouth and lips really get into her flesh. She shivered against him again, and emitted uncontrollable heavy sighs that she was simply unable to suppress. Carol liked it. It was like giving in totally as she'd promised herself she would do.

She pulled her left leg up, leaning it outwards, but Greg stayed on top of her. His wonderfully warm erection had been rubbing up against her all this time and it was a tantalising reminder of what was to come.

His hand moved all the way down her side and went to her left buttock, tightened by her raised leg. She suddenly relaxed a little under him and took his face in her hands. She pulled him down close and kissed him on the mouth, burying her tongue inside him, and playing it around.

He took his hand off her buttock and touched her face again, but Carol grabbed it, pushed it back and slapped it back onto her buttock.

Greg couldn't help but giggle at that.

Carol giggled with him. This was also good fun.

His head was rested against her chest now, through his giggling. He then began to kiss her on the chest. Carol's hands were now on his shoulders and she gently pushed down.

Greg seemed to get the message and he slowly worked his way down to her breasts. He nuzzled against them, kissed, licked and sucked them on the side, and around her nipples, where Carol could feel it most and Carol couldn't help but giggle again. When he was nibbling and playing with her nipple, Carol stopped giggling and just lay there, running her hands through his hair and purring and groaning with satisfaction. She grinned at him without him seeing her. But he didn't need to see her to know the pleasure she was feeling. She could lay here forever, melt into him, become one with him. But time was being good to her and the darkness still seemed eternal. It was as good as forever and the delightful sensations rippled through her body.

Moments later, he moved down even further and buried his face into her stomach.

Her stomach muscles convulsed and rode the pleasure coming through her as his lips kissed her stomach's soft flesh. She adored the way he kissed her and touched her. It was so gentle, but her body responded with incredible intensity. It was the deepest, heaviest feeling she'd ever had, drowning out everything else, including her darkest fears.

This was better than riding a sea of tranquillity, her whole body was being transported to an entirely new plain of pleasurable sensations. It was the crest of a wave rushing right through her, charging and wonderfully insistent, yet at the same time, relaxing, calm, uplifting. Cool and warm. All the pain she had been through suddenly seemed from a different time, something from a nightmare that had only ever been inside her mind, even though she knew it was very real and she'd only managed to escape from it a few hours ago. This pushed the darkness back even further into eternity and distorted time once more it seemed.

As he kissed her, she felt free and excited enough to stretch. She stretched her upper body, lifting her upper body and stomach muscles up towards her and raising and folding her arms above her head, resting them on the soft pillow. She also stretched her legs out as well right in front of her. She stretched her whole body out, loving the feeling of the release in her muscles as she succumbed to the pleasurable sensations at the same time. She sucked air through her teeth and shuddered, a long, delicious shudder which didn't seem to want to stop. Carol moaned.

Carol couldn't help it, she gently turned over onto her left side, happily recovering from her wonderful stretch and she knew that Greg had briefly stopped kissing her, basically allowing her to turn over most probably. (What Carol didn't know however, was that Greg had deliberately stopped to look up at her and smile when she had moaned, after enjoying her shudder). But he didn't stop. Laying on her side now, Carol was shivering, but not because she was cold. Her breathing was very heavy and shaky. She couldn't really believe this was happening. She grinned to herself. She shivered with excitement.

Thankfully, Greg wasn't finished. She was hoping he wasn't. He kissed her arm and her shoulder, stroked it gently and then his hand was running up and down the silky plain of her back, down to squeeze her bottom and then all the way up again, curving its way over her waist and up under her arm, where he stroked her breasts. He pulled his hand back again and slid it right up under her arm, into the warmth of her armpit, which Carol liked, but she knew that Greg was desperate to go somewhere else. Somewhere where he'd wanted to go for so long, but was still hesitant. Carol was desperate for it now too. Her body had experienced breathtaking pleasure, and it wasn't even all the way yet. He wasn't even inside her.

The very thought of that made Carol shudder again.

Suddenly, his hand slid down from under her arm, down her side, dipping into the curve of her waist, round her buttock, and onto her thigh. Carol knew it. He was really heading somewhere now. She sensed it. She sensed it more than she'd sensed anything else tonight. It was finally happening. It really was happening. She could hardly wait. She wanted it and Greg knew it.

Carol felt his hand suddenly moving around her thigh, his own body shivering with anticipation behind her, but he wasn't kissing her a great deal at the moment. His hand slipped right inside her thigh as Carol squeezed her thighs together. It slipped right in between the warmth inside her thighs and between her legs, moving back and forth, to and fro. Carol could feel his breath on her neck and face above her as his breathing got heavier. Carol's also got heavier. She sucked air between her teeth again, harder than before, filling her lungs up and letting the air out raggedly. His hand moved further up, touching her between the legs, where Carol felt so warm and moist and soft. And wet. Carol felt so wonderfully wet and moist down there. He was touching her, rubbing her, and desiring her, wanting her.

Carol lay down on her back and gazed up at him. Greg gazed back down at her, now lying on top. Carol gazed up at him with her mouth open. She breathed heavily into his face, and even in the darkness, she sensed the look in his eyes; a look of breathtaking shock. He couldn't believe it any more than her. Her heart was thumping with renewed anticipation.

Oh my God, she thought in a sudden flash. *This is it.*

They gazed right into each other's eyes, as Greg slipped himself gently inside her, with a little help from Carol. Even in the near darkness, she could feel Greg's responses almost as well as her own. It was incredible.

The larger than life heat of his erection sliding comfortably into the awaiting warmth between her legs was the most erotic feeling she'd experienced all night. After all the feelings she'd experienced up to now, she was amazed she could still feel as excited. She felt so wonderfully wet and moist down there. So warm and hungry. And she enjoyed him being inside her, feeding her hunger.

She spread her legs apart, allowing him more room and she wrapped her arms around him, pulling him down. Carol began to move slowly up and down in response. Rocking her hips against his pelvis. Her legs and arms tightened around him. She breathed hard. Her chest felt pleasantly heavy, and her breasts heaved gently against her, bouncing her nipples back and forth.

She smiled up at him, her mouth wide open, and closed her eyes. Her hands suddenly gripped his shoulders. They were both perspiring lightly. Carol's breathing became harder and sharper, sounding like and eventually becoming sudden gasps, as Greg pushed faster and harder inside her, growing more excited. Pleasurable sensations again began to rush through her; glorious muscular spasms that started between her legs and rippled through her entire body, or seemed to, rippling up through her pelvis and rushing all the way up through her, as if it were heading directly for her head. She'd had orgasms before, but nothing compared to the sudden uplifting and intense pleasures of this. The irresistible spasms came in giant waves and it made her grip him even tighter on the shoulders. And it made Greg move faster still. Her arms suddenly released his shoulders, wrapped around his body and squeezed.

The exciting, eyebrow-raising sensations increased, as did Greg's speed. They increased more and more, literally rippled through her, pulsing, relaxing, pulsing and contracting, gloriously free, as Greg pushed faster than ever. The heat of him inside the large, warm void of her had certainly touched something, the sensations were unlike anything she'd felt before. Perhaps it was the intensity of the night, what it meant and still that fear of what she was doing. Either way, it was definitely happening. Her legs tightened around him, the insides of her thighs squeezing wantingly against his hips, her legs pulling up towards her, as he fell right down on top of her and kept on pushing. She felt wonderfully squashed under him, enjoying the full weight of him on top of her, pressing down on her, it was as if she belonged here forever and there was nowhere to go, and the sensations were going to grow stronger, forever, and there was no stopping them. Her buttocks clenched, her toes curled up, tight, tapping happily against the backs of his thighs, her tummy flapped against his and her hands, which she almost couldn't move, suddenly slapped onto his buttocks and gripped them. She pulled him in further and the sensations strengthened in intensity.

They were tidal waves rushing through her, and there was no stopping them; reaching higher and higher, until there was no higher to go, right up on the crest, ready to conquer the world, but they reached anyway, and Carol felt like her head was going to explode with the thumping intensity of it. She could hardly breathe. His weight on top of her seemed to get heavier all the time and she loved it. She was catching whatever breaths she could, her mouth wide open, and she realised she was making shrieks and grunts of pure delight; such intense, unbelievable pleasure after so many days and nights of pain.

She shrieked louder and louder, knowing that Greg was enjoying her pleasure too, when suddenly she felt something. His buttocks clenched harder under her hands, and he slowed down, dramatically, pushed a few more times inside her and suddenly stopped, his tensed body collapsing into a relaxed heap against her. He'd had an orgasm. That's what she had felt.

Then a frightening thought entered her mind. They hadn't used protection. She could get pregnant. There was always a chance, even if the chance was slim. For a moment, she panicked, but she decided that this night was too special to think about that. This night had been full of irrational and dangerous risks. She would worry about it tomorrow. Tomorrow was going to be a hell of a day. But this was one hell of a night.

Carol held him tight, her breathing beginning to slow down, but Greg's remained quite heavy, blowing against her ear. No matter what her fears were for tomorrow, Carol felt as if she could float freely right up to the roof of Greg's bedroom, and even through the roof, up into the night sky.

She was still riding on the sexy sensations. They hadn't quite stopped, even though Greg had done all that he could do, but she knew she could feel more.

She pushed him over, getting on top of him. She rocked back and forth gently. He was still hard enough inside her to keep the pleasure going. She pulled herself up, liking the surprised, but exhausted look on Greg's face.

She moved him around inside her and squeezed her buttocks forward against him, and relaxed, then squeezed them forward again, and a few pleasant little spasms shot up, tickling through her, making her smile, but that was it. It was more than enough. She just didn't want any of this to end. She collapsed onto him again and hugged him. Kissed him.

Carol still found it hard to believe that she'd had the guts to go through with this, now that they'd made love (wow, had they ever!). She had to go back and face Sean again, no matter what. But she also believed that if this was perhaps her only opportunity to be with Greg, regardless of the grim consequences to face because of it, or the depressing belief that she didn't think she could ever have any kind of permanent happiness with Greg as there was so much in the way of that, then one night like this with him was better than never knowing at all, even if it couldn't last forever. It had certainly been worth it. She knew she had made the right decision. And that at least felt good.

Carol lay on top of him, her head buried into his neck and her hand on his chest. Her breathing had calmed down, and Greg's was beginning to. Carol then felt his arm slip around her and his hand gently patting her on the bottom. Carol smiled to herself and wriggled luxuriously against him. It felt nice. He still wanted her close.

Whether or not it was in response to this wonderful night together, or the fact that it could be their *only* night together, didn't matter. Nothing mattered except for the night, which surrounded the two of them like a protective blanket, shielding them against the harsh realities of the day after to come, along with the moonlit shadows floating around them like ghostly guardian angels.

Even though she didn't want to, even though she wanted to stay awake and be close to him forever, she knew, as Greg did, that peaceful sleep wasn't far off.

And soon, she drifted.

Carol awoke screaming in the dead of night, shooting up from the pillow, awakening Greg suddenly too. It was still dark.

'Carol,' he said, and the room quickly filled up with weak light as he turned his bedside lamp on. He held her firmly around the shoulders.

'Oh, God, I'm sorry, I didn't mean to,' Carol blubbered.

The dream had nearly shattered the peaceful infinity of the dark, but the strange, dreamlike quality, unpleasant though it was, made sure it remained intact.

'Oh, God, forgive me,' Carol blubbered again.

'Shhh, Carol, I'm here, it's okay,' Greg said, sounding fearful for her. 'It was only a dream, I'm here.'

'Oh, God,' Carol said, 'he came storming in here…'

'Sean.'

Carol nodded. 'He was yelling and shouting things at me, out in the street, horrible things. I got up to take a look out the window and I saw him out there. He was in the middle of the street, running up and down, banging on peoples' doors, looking for me and then he saw me in the window and pointed up at me. He came storming up to the door and banged on it, demanding to be let in. I was terrified, I didn't know what to do. I just ran downstairs with nothing on and tried to hold the door in place, I just ran down there and left you up here, I thought he was going to get in. I knew I couldn't stop him. I ran away from the door and ran down the hall, but I heard the door crash in and he stood there and came running in after me. I ran into the kitchen, but it was *our* kitchen, in *our* house, and he started to kick me, and I really felt it and then I heard you come downstairs, in *our* house; you wondered what was going on. I screamed for you and you panicked and tried to help me, but Sean stormed down the hall towards you and hit you so hard you were knocked out. I thought he'd killed you. I screamed. Then he came thundering back towards me, growling and he… he…' The dream was so frighteningly vivid that she'd recalled it so fast, she'd run out of breath, almost choked on her own words. 'He was going to kill me. My God, he was going to kill me. What was I thinking coming here tonight? Jesus, what the hell am I doing here? What was I—'

'Hey,' Greg said, 'hey, hey, hey, listen to me.' He held her face in his hand and looked into her eyes. 'It was just a dream, that's all. You're here with me now. Me, not Sean.' He had an earnest look in his eyes, trying to convince her. 'Carol, have I hurt you in any way tonight? Have you felt anything tonight but pleasure and happiness? Not because of me. It was you.'

Carol nodded. 'It was wonderful.'

Greg grinned. 'I know you're worried about tomorrow. So am I. I'm terrified. But we'll worry about that when it comes. He isn't going to kill you. You're not alone with this anymore. You have me. I'll help you any way I can. I love you, you know.'

Carol made a weak grin. She sniffed.

Greg smiled. 'Hey, I tell you what,' he said, and pulled the quilt right back. 'Lay down on your stomach.'

'What?' Carol said with a frown.

'Go on, lay down. Trust me.'

She did so. She lay flat down on the bed on her stomach. Her legs stretched out behind her.

'Arms by your sides,' Greg said.

She did so. She stretched her whole body out flat on the bed.

'Now don't look around,' Greg said. 'Just enjoy the best massage you've ever had.'

Carol had closed her eyes and she suddenly felt Greg's fingertips running up and down her spine, like they were tinkling on piano keys. She felt them running along her legs, lightly, right down from her toes, where he playfully tickled her, up to the smooth moulds of her calves, and right up to the tops of her thighs, then over the slightly raised crescent of her buttocks, squeezing and delicately pinching them, and on into the arch of her back. Tingles ran through her like tiny electric shockwaves. She shivered.

'Nice,' Carol whispered, smiling. Not being able to see what Greg was doing made the sensations feel stronger. She didn't know what was coming next.

He must have also started from beside her as she hadn't felt him move yet. Anyway, his weight was next to her, not on her. He then pushed her hair aside and kissed her on the back of her neck, which made Carol jerk slightly, but she simply giggled. Another sexy shiver.

She felt him move. His weight shifted, and she then felt him sitting on her legs, astride them. She felt his hands on her sides, under her arms, as he moved them up and down, squeezing gently. He moved them right up under her arms, into her armpit and squeezed continuously. His hands were soft and warm. His fingertips brushed up against the sides of her breasts that were squashed under her. She enjoyed that most of all. She wasn't sure whether to melt into Greg or the bed beneath her.

She was almost half asleep by now. But just then, she thought she heard Greg say something. It didn't matter. It was probably something nice whatever it was.

'That's it, Carol,' Greg said quietly, but he didn't think she could hear him. He was glad she couldn't. 'You just lie there and enjoy it. You deserve it.'

Greg looked again at the marks on Carol's lower back and they made him feel sick. But he didn't look at them any more than he had to. There was no point. Looking at them too long would only make him think about Sean, and that was the last thing he wanted to do. There was going to be plenty of time for that in the morning. Carol had probably forgotten they were there. He concentrated only on making Carol feel good. She had done enough for him tonight. She was one of the most passionate, loving women he had ever known and that mysterious quality she had had shined through.

Making love with her had been extraordinary and he was glad she'd enjoyed it too. By the looks of it, she'd fallen asleep again. He lay back down gently beside her, reached to his left and turned off the lamp and then stroked her back. Darkness again. He was facing the window. He didn't particularly want daylight to shatter the darkness of this extraordinary night either.

*

Carol awoke again in the middle of the night, this time with no bad dreams. The room was still in darkness and shadows, and Greg was sleeping next to her. She grinned at him. She looked out the window, but she didn't want to get up and close the curtains. There was no way she was moving from this position.

Carol awoke again just as dawn was breaking through. The far horizon was a cloud-streaked purple-blue colour. To Carol, it almost looked like a fore-warning of what was to come.

She turned over, not wanting to look at the sky beyond the window. It was an unwelcome sight. She could have got up to close the curtains, but she still didn't want to move from this spot. She wanted to stay beside Greg.

She looked at Greg asleep beside her, lying on his stomach, with his face towards her. She smiled at him and stroked his back, then put her hand on his bottom. She loved him, but she felt sad. The night was no longer endless, the darkness was not infinite. Of course, it never was. It simply *seemed* like it was. It would be morning soon.

But she was with Greg now. And anything could happen tomorrow. With that, she shifted closer to him and snuggled up against him.

★

Daylight. 8 a.m. Greg was the first to wake up. He looked at Carol still peacefully asleep and naked beside him. He smiled.

He got out of bed, rubbed his eyes, put on his dressing gown and then went downstairs to the lounge to gather their clothes up, which they'd undressed out of last night.

The lounge itself was normal room temperature, now filled with daylight as the curtains were still open in here too, and the fire was of course dead. Indeed, the room itself seemed dead, compared to the atmosphere in here last night. The standard lamp was still on. A bit of a waste of power, but what the hell. He turned it off. He gathered the clothes up and then went upstairs to the bedroom.

He put the clothes over a wicker shelf by the window, where he kept a stack of books, reference and some good fiction titles. Carol's briefs were still on the floor, a small reminder of getting into bed last night. The way she'd taken them off; standing there, legs straight, and bending right over and pulling them off, dragging them slowly, provocatively down her legs turned him on even now. He picked them up, grinning, and put them on there too. He had his back to the bed.

Carol awoke. The very real glare of daylight was now on her face. She blinked several times against it and reluctantly opened her eyes to it. But she sensed that she had not woken up alone, which she was thankful for. He was in the room. This morning of all mornings she did not want to feel alone.

She turned around and saw Greg standing near the foot of the bed, by his dressing table. He was fiddling around with something from one of the drawers, which was open. She looked at him standing there in a light-blue robe and she smiled. After last night, it was a pity that he was wearing it. A small snicker escaped her.

Greg turned around and saw her. He smiled, but he was curious. 'Morning,' he said.

'Hi.'

'Feel okay?'

'I'd like to say yes, after last night, but not really. I'm worried about today.'

Greg nodded in understanding.

'What were you laughing at just then?' he asked.

'Oh, nothing, it doesn't matter.'

'No, it does. Please, tell me. I'd like to know.'

'It's nothing really. I was just thinking about last night, that's all, and then I looked at you. I wondered what you looked like from behind under that dressing gown. It's kind of funny thinking about it afterwards. The morning after.'

Greg smiled and nodded. 'I understand what you mean. Last night I mean. You turned me on.'

Carol smiled back. 'You turned me on. You've got a nice body. Nice little bum too.' She giggled.

'Really? Thanks,' Greg said with a chuckle.

Carol lay there, leaning on her elbows, eyeing him up and grinning. 'Greg, take it off,' she said, feeling the sparkle in her own eyes.

'What's that?' Greg said, looking at her.

'Your dressing gown, take it off. I want to get a look at you in the daylight.'

Greg smiled, still with his back more or less towards her and undid his robe. He slipped it off.

Carol felt a nice, warm glow as she looked at him. He looked even better in the daylight. She couldn't help but lick her lips and bite her lip as she looked at his buttocks.

'You do have a nice bum,' she said.

Greg chuckled again, looking at her. 'Thanks. Not as nice as yours though.'

Carol then crawled forward on the bed, and lay on her side across it.

'Are you getting ready for work?' she asked, afraid that she would have to wait all day to confront Sean, when she would rather get it over with.

'Oh, heavens, no,' Greg said. 'I'm not going in today. The business can run smoothly without me for a day. My assistant can take care of things while I'm away. I'll call them later. I'm needed here. Anyway, as if I'd leave you here alone all day with this to worry about. What kind of guy do you think I am?' he grinned.

Carol grinned. 'I was wondering.'

She patted the bed in front of her, wanting him to sit down. He did so. He sat down on the edge of the bed right in front of her. She liked being in close physical contact with him again. She put her hand on his thigh and stroked up and down, close to his genital area. It relaxed her. 'Last night really was amazing,' she said. 'No matter what happens today, I'll never regret it.'

'Me neither.'

'I love you,' she said softly.

'I love you too,' he said back.

'It's amazing how I can feel so strongly about you in just a single day.'

Greg nodded. 'It's probably rare, but I suppose it happens. I fell in love with you almost instantly. After our lunch together yesterday, you were so easy to talk to, so full of charm and so attractive that I just wanted to know more and more about you. You intrigued me. I enjoyed listening to you talk, your voice. The gentleness of it. But underneath, you were so strong.'

Carol lay there listening to him, turned on by what he was saying. She continued to stroke his thigh, wanting to touch his genitals.

'I knew you were afraid, but you tried so hard to fight it. I admired that. And, when we were walking back to my car, just after coming out of the coffee shop, when I asked if I could see you again, the way you stopped and stood there; I'll never forget the sparklingly passionate look you had in your eyes. They looked like they were pure silver, not grey. I just wanted to hold and kiss you right then. But I knew it wasn't the right time.'

Carol grinned at him. Funny how she had thought more or less the same thing at the time.

'You're not the only one,' she said. 'I was also busy picturing you with nothing on.'

Greg gave her a look. Surprise was in there somewhere. Carol simply smiled at him. Greg chuckled. He seemed embarrassed. 'So, now you know.'

Carol made a slight nod. 'Now I know.'

'And you like it?'

'Yes. It gave me enough pleasure last night.'

'I'm glad you like it,' he said, rather blandly.

Carol sensed something wrong in his tone. 'Why wouldn't I?' she asked gently.

'Well, to tell you the truth, I've never really felt that confident about my body,' he said.

'What? I can't believe that,' Carol said. 'You're tall and slim.'

'I see myself as skinny.'

'Skinny? No. You're not skinny. Just slim.'

'I'd rather be bigger. Built that is. I'm not exactly a hunk. And I'd like to be a bit smaller. I never really liked being that tall. I feel I have to be tough, and really confident. And I think I stand out too much as well. I don't think I like that much. I'm a bit of a wimp really,' he said with a chuckle. Carol chuckled too, amused by his subtle confession. 'Especially with attractive women,' he added.

'Well, you seemed confident enough with me yesterday,' Carol said.

'That's partly because of the strong attraction I sensed between us when we looked at each other. Anyway, as I said, I just seemed to feel comfortable with you.'

'Well, I certainly felt comfortable with you last night. I knew it would be good between us, but not like that. It was wonderful.'

Greg grinned. 'I know. I didn't want it to end. But it still seems so vivid. Everything does. Kissing you for the first time by the lounge door. When you almost left.' She grinned at him. 'Sitting in front of the fire, and eventually kissing and taking our clothes off.'

Carol lay there, remembering it herself. The memories were very vivid.

'The way you took your clothes off though, when we were in front of the fire. Did that turn me on! You were such a tease.'

Carol chuckled. 'Well, I couldn't resist it. The mood was right. The warmth of the fire was seductive. It was fun. Taking everything off one stitch at a time, slowly revealing my body to you.'

Greg grinned into her eyes. Carol grinned back into his. A pleasant shiver went through her chest and her nipples swelled again in response. She smiled up at him.

He put his hand on her waist, stroked it up and down her back and pulled it around and up to her breast.

Carol grinned right into his eyes again and sucked air through her teeth and let out a moan. She enjoyed his hands touching the morning softness of her skin.

'I can almost feel the warmth of that fire again,' she said.

The fire. The memory was burned in the back of Greg's mind. It was probably what had helped to make last night so special. But how he loved that memory. It haunted him, but in a nice way. He knew it was real, but at the same time, it seemed almost unreal. It was like something out of a dream, only better.

The first thing he remembered about it was the fire. He remembered at first how it had scared him a little. It was strange. That flickering reddish-orange light under the door and above it in the window. But he would never forget the moment when he secretly, quietly opened the door to see the amazing, beautiful sight that was beyond.

But right now, he remembered it all. From being awoken by the bad dream, to seeing what was in the lounge that night more than twenty years ago, and he couldn't help but smile about it. It was so beautiful. It was well worth telling.

Carol wondered what he was thinking. He was smiling, but his eyes had shifted.

'What?' she asked.

'Oh, it's just something you made me think of, that's all. Something which happened when I was a kid.'

'Oh? What was that?' Carol asked, smiling curiously. 'It's your turn to tell me now.'

'When I was seven years old,' Greg said, 'I witnessed my mum and dad… you know…'

From the look in Greg's eyes, Carol knew what he meant.

Her eyes widened with surprise, and her mouth dropped open.

'Make love? Really? Christ. Well this I've got to hear.' She sat up and wrapped her arms around her knees, but decided that wasn't comfortable enough, so she crossed her legs flat and leaned her arms on them. 'Tell me about it.'

'It happened late one night, gone midnight,' Greg said. 'I'd woken up from a bad dream, which I can no longer remember, and naturally, like any child, I wanted to go to my mum and dad for a bit of comfort.'

Carol nodded.

'So, holding my teddy bear close to me, I went to their bedroom and opened the door, hoping to get in with them for a little while. But they weren't there. They weren't in bed. Their bed hadn't been touched. It was still neatly covered. So, I went and looked in the bathroom and the other bedroom, but I couldn't find them. So, finally, I went downstairs, step by step, and when I got down to the hallway, I saw this flickering orangey-red light under the lounge door and in the window above it. I was filled with a strange sense of wonder. I was instantly intrigued by it.'

'I'm not surprised,' Carol said, feeling a sense of awe approaching. This sounded big.

'I walked towards it, fascinated. It felt like I was hypnotised. Then, I walked right up to the door, and at first, I hesitated. I was a bit scared. I didn't know what it was. I didn't know what was in there. I didn't know what to expect. I was only a kid. Maybe I thought something was wrong, I didn't know. Yes, I think I was a little scared at the time. It felt so strange. Anything could have been in there. I was afraid to open the door. But, I don't know, I think I knew, even as a kid, that nothing bad was in there. And it didn't matter if I opened the door. So I did.

'I reached out, gripped the handle, turned it and pushed the door open slightly, but just a little, only an inch or so. The red light almost filled the room, made it seem bigger, wonderful shadows danced on the walls and ceiling and then I heard this crackling sound. I knew it was the fire, but I also knew there was something else in there. It's almost as if I felt something in there waiting for me. I also knew they were in there. I opened the door a little further, as far as I dared, although I wasn't really afraid anymore for some reason. And then I saw them,' Greg said, in such a powerful tone that Carol couldn't help but be touched.

She blinked and took a breath.

'They were both sitting beside the fire, naked. No television on, not even any music on, just them and the fire,' Greg said, smiling, obviously enjoying reliving the memory. His voice sounded pleasantly haunted.

Carol smiled too. 'Just like us last night.'

Greg looked at her. 'Almost,' he said.

'Pity I had to bring us up here. We could have relived that.'

Greg shook his head slightly. 'I don't think it would've been as good. Your idea was better. More of a turn-on.'

Carol grinned appreciatively. 'I'm sorry, you were saying…'

'My mum was sitting in front of my dad on the rug, her back was towards him. He was kissing and stroking her from behind, kissing her neck and shoulders, stroking her back and arms and her long, dark hair. His hands rested on her shoulders, then they slipped all the way down to her waist and wrapped around her. He held her like that for a moment. She couldn't stop smiling. I think I then remember seeing her push his hands down further, right down inside her legs. She curled up against him, tensed her body up, still smiling. I saw his hands move further down her thighs, then up again, right up in between.'

Carol detected a hint of nervousness creeping into his voice for the first time. But a good nervousness. He was telling her a pretty important moment in his life. She swallowed.

'He started moving his hands up and down there. My, she was enjoying that. I saw her laughing. My dad was smiling. She turned her head to the side, facing where I was standing, peering at them through the gap in the lounge door. Her eyes were closed. She opened them again and looked at him. They exchanged a look.' He paused.

Carol was amazed how he could remember all of these details after so long, but she wasn't surprised. It was amazing what the memory could recall sometimes, especially with memories as powerful as this. She was also amazed how his parents had never seen him. But with him standing in a dark hallway and the lounge in dancing firelight and with what they were doing, it was understandable that they didn't see him.

'My dad then leaned back and lay down on the floor. My mum

turned around and lay down with him. He kissed her on the neck and mouth, he stroked her hair and her back, and put his hand on her bottom. The firelight danced all over them. They almost looked like an animated classic painting. It was amazing. I'd never seen anything like it. It was so warm in there. So wonderfully warm, and relaxing. So relaxing.'

Greg was blushing and perspiring, but he said it almost dreamily, like he was really lost in the haunting memory. Carol could tell now that he probably was. Its haunting effect, just listening to it, was fascinating.

'They turned over then, my dad was above her, between her legs, and—' Greg suddenly realised he was giving away a bit too much, and he met her eyes, but Carol just grinned at him, unembarrassed. '…Well, the rest is obvious. They made love. I stood there, watching the whole thing, fascinated. I couldn't walk away, or close the door. Nothing. I stood there and watched it all the way through, until they'd finished, then I must have gone back to bed. Amazingly enough, neither of them saw me. Maybe, thinking back to it, I was camouflaged by the firelight and darkness. But no. I think they were too busy enjoying themselves. Making each other feel good.'

'Yes, I suppose they were,' Carol said, touched by a sense of wonder. Not so much by the memory itself, but by the way he'd talked about it. 'I was just wondering the same thing. How they didn't see you, but I think you're right. It was dark. The firelight must have disguised you somehow.'

Greg nodded and looked at Carol with a slight frown. 'Do you think I was perverted? Watching them like that?'

Carol gave him a solemn look. 'No, not at all. It's only natural that you wanted to watch. Any child would have. A lot of kids probably think it's revolting that their own parents make love, but I don't think it'd be at all bad for any child to see what you did. I know it must have been strange for you at the time, but as you rightly said, it has an unreal quality to it, like something out of a dream, so it's worth holding on to. Memories like that are very rare, Greg. I'd hold onto it if I was you. Remember it every chance you get. And share it too.' She smiled.

Greg snorted. 'Yes, I've never told anyone about it before. I never even told them I saw them. Didn't dare.'

'I'm honoured you told me.'

He smiled. 'It was worth it.'

'Strange though,' Carol said, 'I'd have thought that would've given you confidence for life.'

'Perhaps so. But it didn't.'

'Did they conceive that night?' Carol asked.

Greg looked at her, visibly impressed, but also a little disheartened it seemed by the question.

'No. I'm an only child,' he said.

'They're still together I take it.'

'Yes, they are. Although my dad suffered a heart attack a few months ago. Almost lost him.'

'I'm sorry.'

'It's okay, he survived. Scared us though at the time of course. Me and my mother. So, how about your parents? Are they still married?'

Carol shook her head. 'Divorced when I was ten. And my father's dead.'

'Sorry.'

Carol just grinned at him appreciatively.

'Do you have any brothers or sisters?' Greg asked.

Carol suddenly looked down and nodded. 'Yeah. A brother,' she said. 'We don't speak to each other much these days.'

Greg obviously realised the subject saddened her, and he didn't want to upset her. 'Sorry, I didn't know you didn't want to talk about it.'

Carol grinned up at him again. 'It's okay,' she said.

There was a brief silence between them. Carol knew what was on both of their minds right now. The subject had simply struggled to surface. But it was right in front of her mind now.

Carol then came right out with it; 'I'm terrified about confronting Sean today. It scares the hell out of me just thinking about it. I dread to think what he's going to do to me.' She started to shiver. Those shivers turned into a shudder, and Carol suddenly didn't feel so good or sexy anymore.

'He won't do anything while I'm there,' Greg said, little knowing about the rather menacing tone in his own voice.

Carol looked at him. 'Actually, Greg, I have to talk to you about that. I don't want you with me when I confront him. I want to do it alone.'

Greg's face suddenly became ashen, it clouded over with shock. 'Carol, you can't be serious. That's crazy. That's practically *suicide*. You know what he could do if you were alone? I'd never forgive myself if I let you do it alone.'

'Greg, I have to,' Carol said, more sharply than she had intended, the fear of it starting to creep in.

'No, you don't, Carol, you—'

'I do, Greg. Look, I appreciate that you're trying to help me, but I must confront him alone, at least to start with. Anyway, confronting him together might be even more provocative, and that won't help the situation. If I do need help, then you can stand by, I'll make sure of it, but I must confront him alone, Greg; at least to prove to him – and to myself perhaps, that I do have some guts inside me. I'll be all right, Greg, honest. Please, trust me.'

Greg dropped his head and looked at her again. Fear for her was in his eyes. Carol knew he trusted her, but that was beside the point. He obviously considered it dangerous. Carol did too in a way. But she also thought about the two of them walking right on in there together to confront him and she didn't like that either. Far too conspicuous.

'I can't believe you want it this way. I don't like it, Carol. I don't like it one bit.'

'I have to, Greg. I want to. As I said, you can stand by if I do need help, okay? Please, Greg.'

He wasn't objecting too much to her plan to confront him alone. Maybe he didn't think confronting Sean with Carol was the best thing to do either. He didn't like her plan. But that was simply because he probably saw it as Carol being put in harm's way. But perhaps it was the best way to do it.

'Greg?'

He shook his head and sighed, then he looked at her. 'If it's what you want, fair enough. But I still don't like it, Carol.'

Carol grinned, gratefully. 'Thank you.'

Greg sat there on the edge of the bed, looking unhappy about Carol's decision, but accepting it nonetheless.

'It would be nice of course if we didn't have to go back at all,' Carol said. 'If we just stayed like we are, never went back to confront him.'

'Like running away you mean,' Greg said with a wry grin.

'The thought had occurred to me.'

'It would be easier I suppose. But in the real world, I don't think either of us could live with that.'

'No,' was all Carol said.

Carol looked at him and then uncrossed her legs. She got up on her knees and moved right up beside Greg on the bed, flicking her auburn hair back. She put her hand on his face and tenderly kissed him. She had only just remembered the bruises.

'What was that for?' Greg asked, grinning.

'I just felt like it,' Carol said, grinning back at him, close up. 'Well, actually, it's more than that. There is something I haven't really thanked you for.'

Greg looked at her, intrigued. 'What's that?'

'Well, it just occurred to me. Not once, since we met yesterday afternoon, have you mentioned the bruises on my face. I admit, that did surprise me. I would've thought that that would have crept into the conversation a lot earlier.'

'It didn't feel right to say anything, even though I wanted to,' Greg said, making that point clear. 'Anyway, I didn't want to mention them, because it would've spoilt the time we had together. Besides, what good would it have done to say anything? They only make me angry. I only wanted to look at what was behind the bruises, a pretty face.'

Carol smiled. 'Thank you,' she said. 'I'm impressed.'

Greg smiled back. But his smile soon disappeared. 'So, what do we do about Sean?' he asked, in a tone of disgust. But his eyes were filled with greater fear. 'Will he be at work?'

Carol grinned wryly and grunted. She shook her head and knelt back down.

'He has a day off today believe it or not,' she said. 'But even if he hadn't, I still don't think he would have gone in. Not Sean. He would've made an excuse. I think he knows that I know that too. Confronting me today is far more important than going to work or anywhere. He'll be there. I can almost feel it.'

'Sounds even more ominous.'

'I'm sorry,' Carol said. 'I didn't mean it that way. I just know how he thinks. I think he knows I'll be back. That's partly what scares me. Ironically enough, we're almost on the same wavelength. If he wasn't so violent or abusive, we'd probably communicate quite well. Maybe that's to our advantage though.'

'Mmm,' Greg said, nodding, forlornly.

Carol grunted, wryly. She didn't really think so either.

'Well at least we don't have to wait all day for him,' Greg pointed out. 'That would've been worse.'

Carol nodded in agreement. 'True.'

'Well, come on, Auburn,' Greg said, patting her on the bottom, 'may as well get showered and dressed eh.' He got up.

'What did you say?' Carol asked suddenly, looking up at him. She moved forward and sat on the edge of the bed.

Greg turned to look at her, frowning. 'I'm sorry?'

'What did you call me just then?' She got up and stood there, naked, looking at him.

Greg appeared to think about it for a moment. She still had a grin on her face, so he knew it was something nice. He stood there, frowning. Then, suddenly, it came to him.

'Oh, Auburn. Sorry, I got a bit carried away. Said it without thinking.'

Carol still looked puzzled.

'It's your hair of course,' Greg said, smiling. 'The loveliest head of auburn hair I've ever seen. Shines even better in the daylight.'

Carol thought about it with a grin. 'Auburn,' she repeated to herself. And nodded. 'I like that.'

Greg grinned down at her, pleased that she liked it.

'Auburn. Yes, that's nice,' Carol said, grinning back at him, sweetly.

Greg shrugged. 'Call it a nickname.'

Carol nodded and smiled. 'Well, thank you, kind sir. A night of pleasure and a nice nickname too. You are spoiling me.'

'You can always give me a silly nickname,' he said.

Carol shifted her eyes for a moment, thinking. After all the pleasure he'd given her, why not?

She grinned up at him. 'The Pleasure Man.'

Simple, silly, but obvious, she thought.

Greg couldn't help but smile. 'The… Pleasure Man?'

Carol shrugged. 'Why not?'

Greg laughed. 'No, that's pretty good.'

'Just for us. Auburn and the… no… Auburn Davis and The Pleasure Man.'

Greg nodded and smiled. 'Good. I like it.'

'Pity it couldn't be Auburn Thompson,' she said.

Greg winced slightly. 'That doesn't sound right.'

'I know,' Carol said. 'Strange that. Well, it's just for this once. Because of the circumstances. It'll give us something to remember it by.'

Greg nodded. 'Yeah. Come on, let's get ready.'

They showered together, holding each other, but hardly a word was said. Both remained silent. Carol even wept a few tears, but the running water soon washed them away and kept them disguised. Holding him like this was nice, but she couldn't help but feel cold inside. The warm running water did nothing to stop her from shivering.

It was coming very close.

The confrontation with Sean, that was soon to come, chilled Carol to the bone. Greg didn't comment on her shaking in the shower. He probably knew she was in no mood to talk. Maybe he didn't blame her. She suspected that he wasn't exactly looking forward to it either.

They held each other very firmly, afraid to let go and terrified of what was to come.

They dressed slowly and quietly in the bedroom, with sympathetic glances occasionally passing between them – Carol hardly wanting to say a word, nor Greg, and they went downstairs for a coffee and to try and eat something. But they hardly ate anything. Carol knew it was silly, trying to put it off, which was really what they were doing, and so did Greg, but they were certainly taking their time, and it was doing them no good at all.

By the time they left, it was well over an hour later.

Greg was amazed that he could keep control of the car so well. No excess speeding or anything. He wasn't at all relaxed. His heart was filled with dread. And he was in no hurry to get to their destination.

Carol was in an even worse condition. She trembled uncontrollably. Her stomach was in a tight, piercing knot, and her heart raced frantically. She tried to keep her breathing steady, but she even found that difficult. For a moment, she thought it crazy that the car was taking her closer and closer and she wanted to turn around. She knew last night couldn't last forever, but she so wished it could've done. But now that the reality of the situation was closer, Carol had never felt so scared about anything in her life.

Greg must have sensed her tension.

'Carol, are you sure you want to confront him alone?' he asked suddenly.

'Yes,' Carol said sharply. 'I have to. But you will be there if I need you?'

'Try and bloody stop me,' he said.

They arrived at the house. Carol's heart suddenly went crazy, pounding away inside her, as if it was more scared than her.

Sean's company car was there, black with white lettering on the doors, sitting there like death's waiting carriage, and Carol couldn't help but stare at it. She was trembling violently all over. She was a mess inside. Tight, twisted, knotted, and nervous flutters were raging through her like panicked insects. All her insides seemed to be everywhere but in their rightful places.

'Well, here we are,' Greg said, staring uncomfortably at the front of the house, just like Carol.

'Christ, I feel terrible,' Carol said.

'I'm not surprised,' Greg said back.

Carol made a very deep, compulsive sigh. It came out unevenly. Her mouth was dry and gritty. For a moment at least, she couldn't move.

'Oh, well, may as well get it over with,' Carol said. She felt unpleasantly hot and nervous.

'Carol, just remember, I'll be there if you need me, okay? The slightest hint of real danger and I'll come.'

'Thanks,' Carol said. She hoped it would work out like that.

She got out of the car and stared at the front of the house. Greg stayed in the car, watching, waiting.

A whole rush of panic-stricken, irrational thoughts raced through Carol's mind as she stood there. What would he do? Was he hiding, waiting? Would he attack her as soon as she got in? If so, was he angry enough to kill her? That thought made her shudder. He probably was.

Oh, Jesus, she thought, and took a deep breath.

More terrified than ever before in her life, she walked to the front door.

Sean was waiting.

He was waiting for her to walk in, which she would do at any moment. He waited, thinking of how much he was going to hurt her. The very thought of it excited and thrilled him. He'd waited all night for this.

He'd been in the lounge for most of the night. He hadn't even gone to bed. He'd taken several naps on the sofa, but he had been awake for much of the night and the dead early hours had dragged on, and he was fired up and ready for her. He'd been fully awake and waiting since nine this morning and now at long last, his patience was rewarded. Sean had seen them arrive almost as soon as they did. He saw the blue car pull up outside and somehow he just knew it was them. Instinct told him. He had seen Carol get out of the car. *His* car. That bastard. How he hated that. The sheer fucking nerve of it. He had also seen her walk towards the front door. She'd looked scared. So she damned well should be.

His whole mind and body was like a furnace. The rage and violence had been building up inside him all night, the pressure building and building, threatening, *needing* to erupt. He still felt like an indestructible machine. He felt capable of anything. Even killing that bitch if necessary. The amount of time it'd been building up inside him made no difference. All that time, with Carol not here, had only served to remind him of how she'd humiliated him. And now she was back. She was within his grasp and he was more than ready for her. Sean knew that she had to come back sooner or later. It was only a matter of time. He wanted her to suffer now, just as he had suffered. He wanted her to suffer now more than ever.

He held a knife. A large bread knife. He'd grabbed it, quickly, after seeing them arrive. A sudden moment of extreme, savage instinct made him grab the knife from the kitchen. He wanted to kill her, but he knew he wouldn't. No. The humiliation of this had burned inside him all damned night and he wanted her to suffer. And suffer she would.

And that son-of-a-bitch if necessary.

He waited and listened for the front door and then he heard it. He heard her walk in.

He grinned maliciously. He was ready for her.

Holding the knife, he waited patiently to give her the welcome she deserved.

'Sh-Sh-Sean?' Carol whispered, almost not daring to speak at all, as she stepped into the hallway. Not closing the door. A glance back, to see Greg getting out of his car. There was an uneasy silence in the house. Except for her breathing.

Could he hear it?

Carol felt as if the very fabric of time, as if the air around her would collapse if she even dared to utter a sound.

Her eyes were everywhere, not daring to stop on any one particular spot for any longer than necessary. She quickly checked behind the front door. Nothing. A couple more steps further.

'Sh-Sean?' she whispered again, a little louder and steadier this time, but her fear had not at all weakened.

She glanced up the stairs, but she certainly didn't go up there. She would be too vulnerable and trapped.

She didn't want to go any further either. She wanted to turn and run while she still could. But she had to go on.

She stepped further into the hallway, expecting Sean to come charging out any moment. With each step, she came closer to the lounge door, which was wide open. Was he in there?

A couple more steps.

Sean waited. Enjoying every minute of it. It wouldn't be long now.

He could still picture the two of them together all night, screwing each other, having a good laugh behind his back. Well, they wouldn't be laughing any longer.

This was what he'd been waiting for.

The knife was gripped in his hand.

Carol approached the lounge. The door was ominously wide open, and inviting. She said his name again, her heart thundering so hard she thought it would explode inside her. She peeped inside, but couldn't bring herself to go right in. She didn't think he was in there anyway. He was somewhere else, waiting. She knew it. She could feel it.

She turned apprehensively and stepped into the kitchen, and was about to say Sean's name again, but was stopped by the sight of what Sean had done in the kitchen. The irrational thoughts she'd had earlier didn't seem so irrational any more.

The dining table chairs had been knocked over, kicked around. They were on the floor as if they'd died. One of them was smashed in the far corner. Broken crockery made an ugly mess over the floor, though a lot of it had been kicked out of the way, clearing some of the centre; probably just something else for Sean to swing his feet at. Surely there wasn't much else to break anymore. She then realised that for the first time she had not been around while this was happening, and somehow, not actually seeing it, only seeing the devastation, made it seem more horrific.

Again, she remembered walking out yesterday evening and she remembered wondering what Sean was doing; probably going out of his mind. She was right. Only now she wished she had been wrong, and she wasn't at Greg's house anymore. She wasn't safely away from here anymore. She was back here, back to face the consequences of her actions, and there was still a sense of rage in the air, threatening to erupt.

For a moment, she forgot that Sean was here somewhere. She had a horrible feeling that he was very near, but she couldn't bring herself to move.

Sean wasn't sure whether he wanted to laugh at her stupidity or explode into another rage for what she had done. In the end he just grinned and stood there behind the door, holding the knife. It was the best and quickest hiding place he could think of.

He wouldn't have minded hiding from her forever, keeping her waiting, but he couldn't wait to see the look on her face.

He pushed the door out of his way and came out from behind it, staring at Carol, whose back was towards him.

He wouldn't have minded plunging the knife right into her back so she would have never known what hit her and it would have been no less than what she deserved.

He took a step towards her.

Carol suddenly realised where he was. She sensed him behind her and whipped around to face him, emitting a shriek, as the realisation of just how much danger she was in hit home. She saw the knife.

Oh, my God, she thought. *He's going to kill me, I know it, he's going to kill me…*

She was amazed that he didn't just come after her. He probably enjoyed this more.

He moved in towards her. Carol backed off, her eye on the knife, wondering how serious he was about using it. He could kill her so easily. There was something terrible in his eyes. A dark glint of madness. Carol was almost mesmerised by it. He looked a lot more dangerous. Walking out on him like that yesterday had definitely pushed him over the edge, and she had put herself into a very vulnerable position, not that she had had much choice in the matter.

'Where have you been?' Sean asked her, with a menacing undertone to his calm voice which made Carol's flesh creep.

She couldn't answer him. She didn't know what to say.

'I asked you where you've been,' he repeated, that eerily calm tone again. He moved in closer still and Carol backed off.

Carol tried to keep her own voice calm, although she could barely speak she was so scared.

'Please, Sean, don't kill me, please, I can explain—'

'You've been with another man, haven't you?'

He still moved another step or two closer towards her. She was more threatened by that than if he had just rushed in and attacked her. This way, she had no idea what he would do. She still couldn't help but glance quickly at the knife. What was he planning to do with that?

'Well, haven't you?'

What the hell did he want her to say? Yes? That would surely set him off. He probably wanted it that way.

'I just saw you, you bitch, pulling up outside in his fucking car.'

Carol didn't know whether he would threaten her all night, to spook her, or beat the hell out of her right now, or maybe worse, so she felt it was better to speak up, perhaps with the idea of trying to reason with him.

He was moving in closer all the time, only a couple of feet or so separated them now. Close enough to stab her maybe.

'I'm sorry, Sean, I had to, you hurt me so much, I didn't know what else to do, I just wanted you to stop hitting me, I wanted things to be the way they—'

A swift, hard slap across the face, which Carol didn't even see coming, knocked her off balance slightly and made her stumble back against the kitchen unit.

'I bet you had a really good laugh at me behind my back, didn't you?' he snarled. 'Did you enjoy humiliating me like that?'

She stood there, with a hand on her sore, burning cheek. The pleasure was gone, now it was the pain all over again. But this time there was another type of pain. There was the pain of the abuse right now and there was also the pain of the pleasure being taken away from her. It was only a memory now, and it almost hurt to remember it. That hurt even more.

He continued towards her again and Carol thought he was going to kill her. The knife remained in his hand, but he didn't look as if he was threatening her with it.

He moved in and slapped her across the face again, and again. They didn't seem like angry slaps. He simply hit her like this because he knew he could. Carol could feel tears coming. She didn't want them to, but they did. She would rather he'd inflicted a quick vicious attack, than to intimidate her and make her feel stupid like this, and she still didn't know what he was going to do with the knife. That scared her even more, than if he'd attacked her with it.

He slapped her again, the knife down by his side. Not only did her face burn, but also the humiliation inside her. He poked and prodded her, not in a playful way, but cruelly, maliciously. He was taunting her.

Greg peered nervously into the hallway, almost afraid to walk in.

He hadn't seen much yet, but he had heard plenty. He'd heard Carol call Sean's name and he also heard something that made his heart sink and his stomach twist. Carol's shriek. She must have seen him. Jesus, he hoped she would be all right. She had left the front door open for him. It was nearly halfway open, so he could hide behind it and peep down the hallway. Good. At least that had worked out.

He heard talking. It sounded like him. He was probably giving her a hard time. Greg plucked up the courage to step into the hall. Slowly, he took a couple of steps more.

Carol was in tears now. Sean's taunts were really upsetting her. She couldn't help it.

'Well laugh at me now, you bitch. Go on, laugh at me now.' He repeatedly tapped her cruelly on both sides of the face. He pinched and prodded her painfully and shoved her back. 'Yeah, not laughing any more are we? You're back home now. There's no place to run now. No fancy boy to rescue you. You're here with me. With big, bad husband. Gotta answer to me now. Haven't you? Huh? Haven't you?'

More prodding and jabbing.

She felt like a pathetic, helpless little girl. It almost took her back to the earlier days in their marriage when Sean had been not so much violent, but verbally abusive. Not that he wasn't violent back then, but the verbal abuse always seemed to set everything off. Cruel, childish taunts whenever he got annoyed. It was like being the bullied child in the playground again at school.

She realised she'd pushed him too far this time by walking out yesterday evening, and he had been left by himself all night to go crazy, but dammit! she wasn't going to feel sympathy for him. What she had done, she had done because she had had no choice. After all the times he'd hurt her, she'd had every right to escape and find something better. She had done nothing to him. She wasn't cruel, or devious in any way, or overbearing or arrogant. She had given him her best and he had turned into a bully all by himself. What they once had was good, sexy, but she almost couldn't bring herself to remember those times anymore. There was only the violence.

She didn't want to have to take this any more. In fact, for a moment, she almost forgot that she wasn't alone this time. Nevertheless, apart from Greg, she wouldn't have minded telling the whole world about her pain right now. Sean's abuse was really getting to her.

His bullying persisted. Poking. Taunts. Prodding.

'Leave me alone!' she suddenly cried out, tears spilling from her eyes down her cheeks, scalding them.

Sean just gaped at her and then he laughed. It was an utterly humourless laugh, full of icy hatred, much like the icily dark madness that was in his eyes. Shining like black ice.

'Carol, poor Carol, you didn't really think you could get away with it did you?' There was no sympathy or understanding in that tone at all.

He suddenly raised the knife to chest height, point up, and Carol's heart jackhammered. It almost seemed to skip a few beats and temporarily stop, as if wondering if it was going to be coming into contact with that unpleasant length of steel. If she ever needed Greg's help, it was now.

Greg was terrified that Sean would suddenly realise what was going on and come storming out into the hallway.

Greg's heart was hammering so hard that he swore Sean must have been able to hear it. A silly, irrational thought, but now was as good a time as any for irrational thoughts. He was also damp with a cold sweat.

He could still hear Sean's voice, and whatever he was saying to her in there was not friendly. He also heard sounds that sounded like slaps. He then heard Carol say something that broke his heart.

'Leave me alone!' he heard her cry, her tone full of despair, and his heart ached for her.

He proceeded closer towards the open kitchen doorway, but at the same time, he wanted to turn and run.

He was terrified of what he would have to confront in there.

Sean grabbed her by the neck, and put the knife to her face. He ran the knifepoint over the skin of her cheek and on the vulnerable areas under her eyes. Carol closed her eyes tight. She felt the vicious cold steel of the knifepoint against her flesh and she was terrified that it was going to cut right into her face at any moment. She wondered if he was capable of scarring her face a little after what she had done. She prayed he wouldn't.

Carol winced against the knife and began to make tiny, whimpering noises that sounded like words. 'No. No. Please. No.'

There was no burning pain yet, so thankfully he hadn't cut her. But the knifepoint was still resting wickedly against her face. She would have begged him if she thought it would help.

'You make me sick, you know that? You must think I'm really stupid,' he said, right into her face. 'Did you think I wouldn't know you'd come back? Of course I knew. I know you. I can practically read your mind. This is where you belong. This is our life. Your place is here. Not out there, but here with me. Whether you like it or not. You are married to me. And if you ever run out on me again, I'll kill you.'

Carol swallowed. She dared not open her eyes, in case he cut her with the knife. Her bottom lip quivered endlessly, her eyes wanted to explode into tears. She sniffed and sniffed.

'Do you understand me?'

Carol couldn't answer him. She felt so bad now, that she simply wanted to escape this terrible nightmare and run away for good.

'*Look at me. Look at me!*'

She jumped so much that she thought the knife would end up cutting her. It didn't. She opened her eyes, which stung with tears and looked at him.

'Do you understand me?'

She nodded reluctantly, knowing he would kill her if she

didn't. She was shaking violently all over.

He then nodded, and pulled the knife away from her. He let go of her neck and then threw the knife behind her, across the counter, where it spun to a rattling stop at the end.

Carol thought he was going to stab her just then, but she was more than relieved to see him do that, regardless of everything else. But she wondered, where was Greg? What was taking him so long? She started to panic. Once again, she felt alone.

Sean just stood there.

Suddenly, Carol felt an awful burning pain flaring up and twisting inside her stomach.

It happened so fast. He moved so fast. For a moment, Carol couldn't breathe. She choked on her own breath, held her stomach and doubled over on the floor in front of her.

He'd punched her so hard and sudden in the stomach that she had been in shock.

She lay on the floor, curled up, and finally, after catching her breath, she burst into tears.

Greg waited by the doorway.

He couldn't believe what he was hearing in there. This was something out of a nightmare. To think that Carol had suffered this for three years. He wondered what other horrors had gone on in here.

He covered his mouth and tried not to cry. He had to find strength from somewhere.

Carol would need him soon.

Carol trembled, uncontrollably on the kitchen floor, as Sean crouched down beside her and looked directly into her eyes. She couldn't help but look at him.

The look in his eyes made Carol feel sick, apart from the pain that was already in her stomach.

'You're never going to see that bastard again. Never. You're never going to see anyone again. You're never going to go out again. Not any more. Things are going to change from now on. I'm going to have to keep tighter control over you. You can't be trusted. But remember what I said, you make me mad again and

I'll kill you. But of course, first things first.'

Carol knew she wasn't alone, thank God, but even so, Sean's words made her heart ache, dully, and feel as if a living nightmare was looking her in the face.

Greg was probably nearby, but he hadn't shown himself yet.

Carol could understand that he was probably scared, but he was no coward. He would show up soon. But of course, the question was, would he be able to help her?

'I bet he was good, huh? Yeah, I bet you enjoyed it. It's nice when you enjoy it. Well, I'm gonna take it away from you. Remove all traces of that bastard.'

Carol knew what was coming next and it repulsed her.

This was similar to the way he had made Carol shudder on other occasions, when he'd sexually assaulted her. The things he said, his tone as hard as steel; phrases like: 'Don't make a sound, or I'll hurt you even more'; 'No one must know about this'; and, 'Don't even try to scream, because no one can help you'. It was like being attacked by someone in the street, or even worse, by someone she knew (albeit that she did, making it a terrifying psychological weapon). With practise, he had gotten better at it… unfortunately for Carol.

He got up and stared down at her.

'Now,' he said, 'take your knickers off.'

He was about to undo his trousers, with the intention of raping her.

Carol was about to reach back under her skirt, to pull off her knickers, when she heard something that filled her with enormous, if only temporary, relief.

'That's enough from you, I think,' Greg's disgusted, but furious voice interrupted from what seemed like a mile away, even though she knew he was only by the kitchen door.

Sean turned around like a shot to look at Greg, who was standing just inside the kitchen doorway. Shock and surprise was in Sean's eyes, but Greg didn't expect to see fear in them, and he was frowning. Not far off from a where-the-hell-did-you-come-from? expression.

Greg just stared at him, filled with rage. A rage he didn't quite know how to deal with. It was like confronting the devil, knowing you were in a dangerously vulnerable position.

So this was Sean. Jesus. He also saw the smashed-up dining table chair and crockery on the kitchen floor, and he swallowed. Greg could understand Carol's fear.

He had waited in the hall, until he felt it was time to interrupt, and after hearing what he just had, knowing what Sean was about to do, now was the time. But stepping into the kitchen, realising what he was getting into, had been a nerve wracking moment, and he almost wished he could've gone through with his own plan, both of them confronting Sean.

He had heard a lot of what Sean had said, and it made his heart feel like a chunk of ice, and turned his stomach upside-down. But he was glad at least to have made it inside. It might not have worked out that way. He looked at Sean, who was only about six or seven feet away, staring straight back at him.

He possibly wasn't six-feet tall, but he was big in build, certainly bigger than him. He had powerful dark eyes and a strong face, with a certain boyishness to it, which gave him an unsettling devilish charm, and his very short dark-blond hair, which was thinning at the front, was almost challenging.

'Oh, and what are you gonna do, huh? Stop me?' Sean snorted at him, scowling. 'Get out of my house and mind your own bloody business.'

Greg huffed. 'I think me and Carol spending the night together last night makes it my business,' he said softly, scared that he would provoke Sean.

Sean suddenly glared at him. 'So you're the bastard who screwed my wife?'

'A charming way of putting it,' Greg said, his heart thundering. 'But yes, I was with Carol last night.'

Greg didn't want this to get out of control and he certainly didn't want to provoke Sean into any violence, but he had a feeling there wasn't going to be much chance of keeping this situation under control. Not with someone like Sean to deal with. He quite thought that Sean would attack him now, but he didn't. Maybe he didn't think it was necessary yet, as he could sense Greg's fear.

'Does it give you a kick to screw another guy's wife?' Sean spat.

Greg stood there, shaking. 'Does it give you a kick to beat her up like that?'

'She's getting *exactly* what she deserves for what she did! You think you can run off with her for a night and get away with it?'

'You've been giving her treatment like that for years,' Greg retorted, immediately, even if it was in fact just under three years they'd been married.

'What we do in our marriage is none of your damn business,' Sean shot back, bluntly.

'*Marriage*?' Greg cracked in disbelief. 'This isn't a marriage. How dare you call it that! A marriage is a loving couple. All I see is some violent *thug* beating up his wife.'

Tears of outrage were building up in Greg's eyes. He also had a powerful, if unpleasant feeling of violence raging up inside him. He wasn't a violent man, not by any means. He didn't remember ever having a real fight at all at any time in his life. However, he sensed violence looming ominously on the horizon right now, and it scared him. He didn't like violence, and he certainly didn't want to get involved in it, but he knew there was no escaping it here. He would try desperately to avoid it if he could, although he knew deep down that he wouldn't be able to.

Sean suddenly stepped away from Carol and walked towards him.

Carol had felt such relief when she had heard Greg at the doorway, and it was strange to see Sean turn away from her and turn his attention towards him. This was the first time that she had ever had any help, and although it felt good for a moment, she still felt that she had put Greg in a position which endangered him and she still felt a burning hint of embarrassment about involving him at all.

But from what she saw, Greg stood up well and he tried desperately to keep Sean's attention, stop him from attacking her again. That took some guts – which Carol couldn't help but admire, but she also saw how afraid he was. He looked terrified. And that strengthened her guilt.

However, Carol was well aware that Greg wouldn't be able to

hold Sean's attention forever, and there was every chance that this would all end in violence eventually and it didn't stop her from being afraid for herself or Greg, because there was nothing that she would be able to do about it.

It also wouldn't stop Greg from being hurt either, seriously hurt. That was what she truly dreaded at the moment.

Greg didn't want to feel threatened, even with Sean's nastily menacing, fists-clenched-approach, but he did. And that wasn't going to be of much help to Carol. But right now, this was his problem. He swallowed, and it felt very dry.

Greg was a couple of inches taller than Sean, but his build was nowhere near as strong. He was very slim, hardly at all muscular, and he certainly wasn't fight material. Sean, however, *was* strong, and his strong, firm build was well up to a good scrap. And Greg knew he was nowhere near a match for him.

'I told you it was none of your fucking business, you lousy punk. Now get the hell out of here before I throw you out,' Sean barked at him.

He wasn't threatening Greg with any flying fists yet, but he was moving towards him and pointing the finger and so the threat of violence coming from him was uncomfortably strong.

'I'm not leaving here without Carol,' Greg said back, firmly.

'Oh yes you fucking well are. You'll get out when I say so. Now piss off.'

'Not without Carol,' Greg said nervously.

'I said piss off.'

'You just leave Carol alone. Don't touch her again.'

Sean grinned coldly. 'And if I don't?'

'I'll kill you.'

Greg wasn't really sure why he made such an irrational and exaggerated threat, he knew he couldn't carry it out. But, with such a threatening atmosphere of violence building up here, he had to at least try and be taken seriously, even if the odds were totally against him.

Sean sniggered. 'Sure you will.'

'I mean it.'

He looked Greg up and down and grinned coldly into his eyes.

'By the looks of you, buddy, I don't think I'll have any problems sorting you out,' he sneered.

Greg shook his head in disgust. 'My God, to think that Carol once loved you.'

'She still does.'

'Wrong. Not any more.'

'So why did she come back to me then?'

'She had no choice, that's why. If she had, do you think she would have come anywhere near here?'

'Yeah, well she's here now. Where she belongs. Now, I'm not telling you again, get out, or I'll remove you myself.'

Greg felt a slight sinking in his stomach. He knew Sean was perfectly capable of doing that. But, as Sean turned away from him, Greg bit back immediately.

'You hurt her again, and I'll call the police,' he said, as confidently as he could, or at least enough to sound convincing. He hoped he did. 'I'm sure the police will be very interested to know what's going on in here.'

'Like hell they will,' Sean grunted.

'Oh, I'm sure they will. Physical assault for example.'

Sean just sniggered. 'Married couples always fight. They won't give a shit. Believe me.'

Greg suspected there that Sean knew something he didn't, which wouldn't surprise him, since Greg wasn't exactly familiar with this situation. He could have a point. Maybe the police got calls like this all the time, but were powerless to do anything. Even with him as a witness, it probably wouldn't help. He hadn't actually seen anything yet. And she was Sean's wife, tough as that may sound.

'And there's the sexual abuse. She's told me about the rapes.'

'*Rapes*?' Sean suddenly shot round, looked at Carol and then looked back at Greg. He burst out laughing. 'How can a husband rape his own wife? We had sex! And she bloody loved it. Just like before we were married.'

'You raped her!' Greg yelled at him, uncompromisingly. It was the first note of anger that had crept into his voice. 'Being her husband doesn't give you any more right to force her,' he added.

'Hey, go fuck yourself, you slimy son-of-a-bitch. I'll do what the hell I want with her. This is my house. Now get out before I break your fuckin' neck!' Sean fumed arrogantly, sounding as if he was beginning to lose his patience with Greg.

Greg grunted, and shook his head. This really wasn't getting him anywhere. But he couldn't think of any other way to help Carol.

Sean just glared at him, unimpressed, threatening to move in on him, but also threatening to turn away from Greg and head for Carol again at any moment.

Greg certainly didn't want that to happen.

Carol lay on the floor feeling so goddamned helpless. She almost wished she was fighting this by herself at the moment, instead of involving Greg. The guilt was burning and burning inside her.

She wanted to get up now and grab Sean, claw him to pieces and escape while she had the chance, but she lay there instead, waiting. This would end in violence soon, it was coming closer and there was nothing she could do to stop it.

But the worst thing right now, was her fear for Greg. He was going to get hurt by this soon, she just knew it. And in a sudden flash, that dream came to mind where she thought that Sean had killed him.

Her fear for him doubled.

★

Greg was trying to hold Sean's attention, but he was also speaking from the heart as well.

'I really don't understand what you get out of it,' he said. 'Does it make you feel powerful or something? Beating your wife whenever you feel like it? Abusing her? Marriage is just a convenient weapon for you, isn't it? You're given someone really special and you treat them like that. I just don't understand why.'

'Shut up!' Sean barked, so viciously, he made Greg jump. He wasn't about to explain himself to Greg. 'I don't give a shit what you think. You've said quite enough. Now, for the last time, get the hell out of my house. This is between me and her. It's none of your business.'

Sean turned away from Greg, uninterested and approached Carol again, who was still on the floor. She hadn't moved. Even when Sean was turning towards her, she didn't move.

Greg refused to leave. But he didn't want this to end up in a fight. He wasn't sure if he could handle that. So, he wanted to grab Sean's attention. Divert him from Carol. His mind worked quickly again, otherwise, he knew that Sean would have definitely attacked Carol right there in front of him.

'Carol wants a divorce,' he said, quickly, strangely intrigued by the reaction he'd get.

Sean stopped, turned and looked at him again. He laughed, a lot louder than before, obviously unable to believe what he'd heard. 'What? A divorce? Go to hell you stupid jerk! She's getting nothing of the sort!' he yelled, sounding rather amused and turned back to Carol again.

'Oh, yes she will,' Greg said, realising he was now wasting his time, which meant trouble. 'I'll make sure of it. Carol isn't alone anymore. She has me. And if I have to, I'll fight for a divorce with her every step of the way. Believe me.'

'I thought I told you to get the hell out you wife-stealing creep,' Sean rapped, glancing at Greg again, ignoring his mild threat.

Sean went over to Carol again, who hadn't moved at all from her original position. That hadn't particularly worked quite as well as Greg had hoped. But seeing Sean approach Carol again with his fists clenching up, made Greg panic. Sean wasn't listening to him anymore. Greg didn't know what else to do.

Carol knew this would happen, it was sadly inevitable, but the worst thing about it at the moment was the fact that Greg was here to see it.

'Sean, no! Don't! No, Sean! Please, don't!'

It was more of a plea to Sean this time, not to hit her in front of Greg. Carol knew that Greg wasn't going to be able to stop him anymore, and this was doubly humiliating for her. She didn't want Greg to see her in such a pathetic and desperate situation. But there was nothing more that he could do.

She hated Sean for this.

Greg looked on in absolute horror. Sean was going to beat her again – with him standing there watching.

'Don't even think about it you son-of-a-bitch,' Greg warned him, angrily stepping forward, but fear was his stronger feeling, hence the hesitation. He couldn't believe this. Sean was actually going to beat her right there in front of him.

Sean ignored him completely, and bent right over Carol. She was still screaming feeble protests, which did nothing to dissuade Sean. He pulled his fist right back over his shoulder and swung it hard across Carol's face.

Carol knew this would happen from the start. Sean stormed towards her, totally ignoring Greg and pulled his fist back to punch her. She screamed for him to stop, but it only seemed to make him more angry.

He bent right down over her, and punched her across the face, and a sharp, burning pain exploded through her cheek and lips and seemed to blur her vision a moment.

She looked away from Sean now towards the floor, but she heard and saw Greg lose his own temper and go for Sean.

She felt for him so much. She so wished that he wouldn't. He was going to get hurt.

Greg clicked. The anger inside him was too strong to contain.

'You bastard!' he yelled in disbelief, and marched furiously towards Sean.

His fists were clenched, and he hoped his anger would give him the extra strength he required, and would definitely need.

Sadly, that wasn't to be. Sean must have obviously sensed him coming. He turned fast and landed a devastatingly accurate punch across Greg's jaw, as Greg was sent sprawling to the kitchen floor with a loud cry of pain.

He heard Sean huff contemptuously. 'No trouble,' he heard him say.

Carol couldn't even look. She turned her head right away and began to cry. This was horrible. She felt so embarrassed for Greg, for having to involve him in this.

He hadn't stood a chance. Seeing Sean turn away from her and punch Greg as he tried to help had almost hurt her as much as him. She had only just seen Greg storming towards Sean, but she hadn't looked away for that long and she only managed to look away again after he collapsed to the floor. She wished she could have looked away quicker.

She glanced at him again, hoping that he would be all right. She was thankful that their eyes didn't meet across the floor in a painful understanding. She didn't particularly want to see what was in his eyes. It might have been hate.

He looked in terrible pain.

Right now, she wished she could help him, but Sean came towards her again.

Greg lay on the floor, nursing his jaw. That was the first time he had ever been punched so badly. This was his first real taste of violence. And it was becoming a nightmare.

He looked up to see Sean going for Carol again and he got painfully to his feet. Tears of pain and outrage were building up in his eyes, although he refused to let them out. Therefore, they stung his eyes.

'You bastard,' he grunted, just as angry for the violence directed to him now, as for the pain that Sean was putting Carol through.

He clenched his fists again and made another move towards Sean, hoping to be successful this time.

But yet again, Sean was ready for him. And he was becoming more impatient. He turned away from Carol and grabbed Greg by the collar of his shirt, blocking his punch at the same time. He stared into Greg's eyes.

'You just don't know when to quit, do you?' Sean barked into his face, forcing Greg back.

Greg's look of pure hate meant absolutely nothing to Sean, that much was obvious from the hateful blackness that was in Sean's eyes.

'I told you this was between me and her! But you just had to interfere, didn't you? Well now you're gonna get exactly the same!' He punched Greg, twice, without warning, into the stomach. Greg grunted with pain. Sean then held Greg upright, pulled back and punched him in the mouth, sending him collapsing to the kitchen floor for a second time.

Sean grinned, amused. He was enjoying this, especially when he thought about how the two of them had humiliated him; the thought of the two of them together still filled him with rage. He knew he was unstoppable. He felt such power. He knew they didn't stand a chance. This was almost too easy.

'Sean, stop it, please!' Carol begged him. She couldn't stand seeing Greg hurt too.

'Hey, it's not my fault,' Sean snapped. 'He started it!'

Greg was still on the kitchen floor, his mouth bleeding from Sean's punch, and his jaw throbbing where Sean had hit him before. He felt weak, and his legs felt heavy. He was not in the best shape for this, but he knew he would have to toughen up or he'd only make it worse for himself. He certainly didn't want Carol to see him like this. And he wasn't going to leave totally humiliated after being badly defeated by Sean. That certainly wouldn't help Carol.

He got up and charged for him again, but this time with his head down.

Sean anticipated it as usual, but he couldn't land a decent punch, as this time, Greg went straight in to Sean's chest and forced him back into the kitchen unit, treading on a few bits of broken crockery, which made brittle crunching sounds under their feet. Sean's back dug into the edge of the unit, which Greg hoped had hurt him at least a little. Greg punched him in the stomach as hard as he could. But Sean's stomach was a lot tougher than Greg's and it didn't seem to hurt him much, and Sean was able to grab Greg by the shoulder, pull him up and punch him in the stomach. Greg knew exactly what was coming, and he tried to stop Sean from getting a punch in. He didn't want to be hit in the face again, and he ended up in a grapple, trying to hold Sean back and stumbling slightly as he tried to keep his balance. But Sean's arms were much stronger than Greg's, and he was able to knock Greg's arms out of the way and punch Greg in the face. A horrible burning pain, which seemed to come out of nowhere, flared up through his nose, as he stumbled back and to his left, into the dining table. He knocked against one of the upturned dining table chairs, causing that to make one last little squeak along the tiled floor. Blood trickled warmly down his top lip. It was obvious his nose had been hit, but a more accurate punch from Sean might have broken it. Thankfully, he didn't think that was the case. Sean had not been in a good enough position to do that.

However, Greg was still in pain. He attended to his sore nose and blinked a few times, his eyes watering from the unpleasant burning behind them, and he noticed a small cut on his hand and he wondered where it had come from. But right now, he didn't care, as he leaned against the table, at least thankful to that for stopping him from collapsing to the floor again in a pathetic and humiliating sprawl.

Carol still couldn't look. Although, she knew Greg was still on the receiving end.

'Please, Sean, stop it!' she cried, glancing up at him. He was nearly to her side now and a little closer to her.

'Shut it!' Sean snapped again, as he stood there, waiting for Greg's next attack.

She saw Greg leaning against the dining table. He looked in agony.

'Please, Greg, don't do it. It's not worth it.'

Sean turned to face her. She was now down on the floor to his left. 'I said shut up!' he yelled, pointing at her. 'One more fucking word out of you, you unfaithful bitch, and I'll start giving you the same treatment as I'm giving your boyfriend here!'

Greg looked at Sean standing there and a tiny flash of inspiration came from nowhere, as Sean pointed down at Carol. He was also thankful to the dining table for breaking another fall, although it might not have made any difference. He was thankful to Carol for diverting Sean's attention for just that brief moment. And he was also thankful to whatever it was for giving him that split second flash of inspiration which he had needed. This was his only chance to help Carol and he had to carry it out successfully.

He went for Sean again. He didn't go in low, and he didn't go in with a punch.

Sean waited again, but this time, he did not anticipate correctly.

Greg went in, and swung his foot as hard as possible, right up into Sean's groin.

Sean suddenly made a thunderous, strangled cry of pain; his hands shot to the damaged area and his eyes gaped wide open, looking shocked and full of agony for the first time and he stumbled back against the kitchen unit, his back hitting the edge. He looked in real pain. His eyes closed up tight and he made a strangled noise and began to cough.

Carol looked up at them, amazed. She couldn't believe what Greg had just done. He'd almost done it. He'd actually hurt Sean, and he could put a stop to this before it went any further. She almost dared to hope they could come out of this.

A huge, but bizarre sense of relief, excitement, and fear swept over Greg at that point, as he looked at Sean. It seemed almost unreal that he had a chance to come out of this safely with Carol. But it wasn't over yet, Greg knew he had to finish it off, but he knew he had to be fast. Sean wouldn't stay out of action for very long, and he had to attack while he had the chance.

He went in again; his eyes burning with rage, and his nose, lip and mouth warm and bloody and an ugly bruise which he could feel beginning to develop on his jaw. And then, with his shirt half-hanging out, and with perspiration pouring down his face, which had now gone a very high colour and felt as if it was on fire, he swung his fist right back, with a loud, anguished growl, and landed a punch, a pretty decent one, across Sean's face.

The contact felt strangely good, although he certainly would not have wanted it to come to this, and his knuckles would most likely be heavily bruised. His hand was sore now.

Sean went down. Still in pain from Greg's initial attack.

He made another strangled cough.

Greg looked down at Sean, fists clenched, waiting to see if he would have to do any more to defend himself, waiting to see if

Sean was only trying to fool him and would suddenly get up and attack him again. But he didn't. He stayed down. Greg looked down at him as if this wasn't really happening. Thankfully, his single blow had done the trick. But after what Carol had told him, he wanted to kick Sean again and again, and make up for all of the pain that Carol had suffered over the years, but he couldn't. Not even Sean had kicked him while he was down. But even if he had, Greg still wouldn't have done so. Sean was in enough pain. And, shamefully or not, it was a pleasure for Greg to see.

Carol was now getting to her feet, looking on amazed but saddened. She felt responsible for all of this. And she couldn't help but feel guilty, whether it was for involving Greg or even for hurting Sean, she didn't know. But it was mostly for involving Greg, the guilt for walking out on Sean festered somewhere in the back of her mind. She hadn't wanted it to come to this either, although it had been inevitable.

She walked up to Greg, feeling cold inside.

He was still standing there, scared that Sean would recover and get up and fight back, but Carol knew that that wasn't going to happen.

'Yes, it hurts doesn't it? That's exactly what Carol's had to put up with over the years. Endless pain. I'd like to give you a hell of a lot more, believe me, but I can't,' Greg said bitterly down to Sean, but Carol guessed that all he really wanted to do was get the hell out of there, like she did. He looked sick over what had just happened, but he still wanted to say his piece. 'I may not have been much of a match for you, but at least I was able to give you a taste of what it's like. Which is more than Carol ever could.'

'Greg, please, let's just get out of here. There's nothing more we can do now,' Carol said, tugging him by the arm.

Greg wiped his bloody nose and mouth with the back of his hand and glanced at Carol. He nodded slightly and walked out of the kitchen with Carol, cradling his sore hand. The guilt swelled more inside her, like a black fungus.

'Are you all right?' Carol asked.

'Not particularly,' Greg said. 'How about you?'

'Oh, no better than you I suppose.' She was silent for a

moment, then she said; 'Greg, I'm so sorry about all this.'

'Hey, it isn't your fault,' Greg said. 'You don't have anything to apologise for.'

Nevertheless, Carol felt she did.

They both walked out to the car, still no better off than when they had come.

They arrived back at Greg's house at just after eleven, and both of them were in a pretty grim mood after the violent confrontation with Sean.

Greg had bathed his cuts and washed his face, as did Carol, both sharing the bathroom. Greg also had a small plaster on his hand, where a piece of broken crockery had cut him.

They sat on the sofa, huddled together, cuddled up, but neither of them had talked much up to now. Greg's television and stereo were silent again. They were both afraid of their future together. If any. Thankfully, they had survived the worst of it, the confrontation; Greg said he was just relieved to have been able to help Carol at the last minute, but it hadn't gone exactly the way either of them had hoped. They hadn't gained anything from it.

'Greg,' Carol said suddenly, 'what are we going to do?'

'I don't know,' Greg replied, looking directly ahead.

'I still want the divorce.'

'I know,' Greg said.

'We'll just have to go about it a different way, that's all. My way didn't really work. I definitely want to go through with it. I've made up my mind, Greg, it's you I love, I can't go back to Sean. I don't care what it takes.'

There was a moment's pause.

'There is something I can do,' Greg said. 'It's the only way.'

Carol suddenly turned to look at him, sitting up straight.

'What?'

'I have to go back,' Greg said.

Those words totally shocked Carol. She couldn't believe he would even consider it after what had happened.

'Greg, no. No, you can't. That's crazy.'

'I have to. I have to go back and talk to him alone. Yes, I have to let talking do the work this time.'

‘Greg, there has to be another way.’

‘I’m afraid there isn’t,’ Greg said, glancing at her. ‘And I think you know that.’

‘But look what happened earlier.’

‘It won’t be like that this time.’

‘I don’t like it, Greg.’

He looked at her with a wry grin. ‘As I recall, I didn’t like the idea of you confronting him alone either.’

She gave him a tongue-in-cheek, narrow-eyed, oh-you’ve-really-got-me-there-haven’t-you? look.

‘We have to do it my way now. I have to see him alone. You’ll have to stay here.’

‘What if it doesn’t work?’ Carol asked.

‘It has to,’ was Greg’s rather despondent reply.

But Carol still didn’t like it.

When Greg arrived back at the house, the ugly and violent events of earlier on seemed to play themselves back in his mind, in sickeningly vivid detail.

As he approached the front door, he expected Sean to come charging out with his fists flying, every step he took. But that was only in Greg’s mind. He walked right up to the door, knocked and waited.

Nearly a moment went by and Greg was about to knock again, when Sean came to the door, holding a can of beer and saw Greg standing there staring at him, rather intently.

Thankfully, Sean made no threatening moves with his fists, as Greg had anticipated, he just stood there, staring back at Greg. He had a small discoloured mark on his jaw where Greg had punched him, but otherwise, he didn’t even look as though he’d been in a fight, either an hour ago or at any other time.

‘What the hell do you want?’ he demanded, flatly. ‘Come for another round ’ave you?’

‘No, I haven’t. I’ve come to do something you may have a bit of trouble with. Talking.’

Sean made an amused, but contemptuous grunt. ‘I’ve got nothing to say to you.’

‘Well, I’ve got plenty to say to you.’

'Well, that's just tough. Now piss off,' Sean snapped, rudely, about to shut the door in Greg's face.

'You know you may as well hear me out,' Greg said quickly. 'What I have to say, might interest you. What have you got to lose?'

Sean just looked at him. Greg looked right back. Sean seemed to doubt the intent in Greg's eyes, but the doubt was replaced by curiosity. Maybe there was something in Greg's voice.

Sean then turned away from him, left the door and walked back down the hallway. 'Make it quick, I haven't got all bloody day.'

Greg grinned behind Sean's back and walked in and, just for the satisfaction of it, slammed the front door behind him. He followed Sean into the lounge.

Greg stayed at the door, as Sean slumped down into his chair. He sat back and took a swig of beer while watching television.

Greg stood watching him, just inside the lounge doorway.

'Well?' Sean jumped.

'Carol still wants a divorce. She won't change her mind.'

'And I already told you, she ain't getting one.'

'Oh, come on,' Greg said, 'you don't love her anymore. That's pretty obvious.'

'She's mine and I'm keeping her,' Sean said flatly, after another swig of beer.

'Oh, why? So you can carry on hitting her whenever you feel like it? Well, that's a great defence. Marvellous reason to keep the marriage going. I shouldn't think we'll have too many problems then.'

Sean looked at him, warily. 'What the hell are you talking about?'

'Well, Carol's going to file for a divorce even if you do refuse. She'll probably be seeing the solicitor as soon as possible. Maybe even tomorrow morning. If she has to, she'll drag you through the courts for as long as it takes. And I'll be by her side all the way. We're both prepared to fight for it.'

Sean sniggered. 'Well, if it's a fight you want, then you've got it,' he said. 'I'm not afraid of a long, hard legal battle. Carol's an adulteress. You two won't stand a chance.'

He took another swallow of beer.

Greg grinned, wryly. 'That's where you're wrong,' he said. 'You know, I may not be much good with my fists, but when it comes to courts and legal stuff, I'm a lot better at it than you think. Believe me.'

'What are you, a lawyer?'

'No, I'm not a lawyer,' Greg said, 'I'm just an ordinary businessman. But a very good one. I've also got connections. One of them, is a very good lawyer. A personal friend of mine. He'll be more than happy to help me with this. He's won cases like it before. Carol will have a lot of help on her side and with my support, she'll come through it a hell of a lot better than you. I'm afraid you're the one who won't stand a chance.'

Sean looked at him and eyed him up hard. 'Is that a threat?'

'No,' Greg said, 'I'm just telling you how it'll be. Carol still has some bruises on her body, which are in the process of healing, but I should think the solicitor and the… connections I mentioned, will take one look at them and make up their own minds.'

Sean grinned. 'They'll probably think you did it.'

'Don't be ridiculous. The old bruises have been there for a hell of a lot longer than she's known me. And she'll swear that I never laid a finger on her. Which is true of course. You, however; I bet the hospital records will make for very interesting reading. She couldn't say anything about it before of course, what could she do about it? But now – as I said – she's got me. She's not afraid to say what you've done to her anymore.'

'Hospital records won't prove a damn thing. They were purely accidents, nothing I did,' Sean said, noncommittally.

'Oh, I shouldn't think Carol will have any trouble convincing them, or a court for that matter, that the numerous hospital visits for quite serious injuries were down to *your* physical abuse. She'll tell them everything. Even about the sexual abuse. But it's the physical abuse we'll really go for. And I was a witness to what happened this morning. I'll tell them all about that too.'

'You started it, you tried to attack me.'

Greg huffed wryly. 'No, I was trying to help Carol. But I don't think I'll have to try too hard convincing them of that. And as I said, with the very good lawyer that I shall provide Carol with, I shouldn't think we'll have any real problems.'

Carol sat on the sofa alone, wondering what the hell was going on over there. She didn't think they were going to fight again, but many other things could be happening. She just hoped that Greg could convince Sean about the divorce.

Greg obviously knew what he was doing, but this waiting left plenty of room in her mind for doubts.

Sean studied Greg, warily, trying to search for the slightest hint of a crack in his confident exterior. But Greg knew he couldn't find any yet. Greg remained absolutely stern, and Sean must have forced himself to look away. Maybe to make Greg think he was just uninterested. At least Greg hoped so.

'You see,' Greg added, wanting to catch Sean's attention again, but he was careful not to sound too over-confident, 'you may be able to get a pretty good lawyer on your side. And you have the adultery perhaps, but I do think Carol's case is a lot stronger. Of course, I know it'll be very difficult for us too, but we'll have a lot of help and support on our side, especially my family, and neither of us are afraid of a long, hard divorce either, if that's what it takes; I think it'll only succeed to make us stronger and pull us closer together. Then there's the costs to consider. But money is no problem. No matter which way you look at it, I can't think of a single reason why we shouldn't come through this. But I honestly don't see what you're going to get out of it. Apart from a lot of wasted time and money.'

'You sound as if you know everything,' Sean snapped.

'We've had time to think this over,' Greg said, confidently, lifted up inside by the strength of what he was saying. 'But I don't think you have. It's an empty threat with you, you've done it deliberately, just to waste our time. But it'll be yours that's wasted. Carol's still with me. There's no children involved, so it'll be even easier for Carol. If it's a long, hard divorce you want, so be it. We're not afraid. We've got nothing to lose. Have you?'

Sean turned to him and studied him hard. 'You're bluffing,' he said.

'Bluffing?' Greg said, amused. 'We're not playing a game of cards, Mr Davis. And you know I'm not.'

Greg stood his ground and remained stern, which was getting easier.

Sean was silent, uncertain. He didn't stop studying Greg, hoping that studying him for long enough would make Greg uncomfortable, force him to show his doubts, which it didn't, as Greg was more than prepared to do this the hard way, as was Carol, even if they would rather not. Sean then turned away again and looked at the television.

Greg didn't want to show any disappointment, so he simply decided to leave it there.

'Suit yourself,' he said, and immediately walked out.

Sean sat there, uncertain, as Greg walked off, starting to wonder if he was doing himself any favours. He had another drink of beer.

It would've been nice and enjoyable putting those two idiots through a bitter, hard divorce, give them what they deserve, make it as difficult as possible for them, but would it be that hard for them? He didn't want to believe Greg, all that stuff he'd said about his lawyer and everything else, but for some reason, he did. That creep was probably the type who might have a good lawyer. Besides, he was a little too confident and eager for Sean's liking. Maybe Carol wasn't even worth it. She had more than enough to remember him by. They wouldn't last. He continued to think about it though.

As soon as Greg walked down the hallway towards the front door, he wanted to go back again and wait for Sean to agree.

He was pleased with his performance in there, hopefully one which worked, but he felt incredibly anxious and not particularly in a rush to leave. The way Sean had looked away from him; did he really think it was a bluff? Did he really believe all that? Greg had sounded convincing, and he was pleased that he hadn't let himself down, but was it convincing enough? Greg didn't underestimate Sean by any means. He had said and done all he could to make Sean see it from their point of view, but had he done enough for Sean to change his mind? The question prodded at his mind again and again, even though there wasn't really much more he could have said.

Greg got to the front door, grabbed the handle and opened it.

That's when Sean's voice suddenly stopped him.

Greg's heart almost skipped a beat.

'Hold it!' he heard Sean yell from the lounge.

Greg froze, swallowed, his throat grittily dry, and he turned around to look at him, blandly. But deep inside Greg was a churning anxiety, which made his stomach tighten and his heart race. His mouth had a metallic taste. But he didn't dare show any emotion like that to Sean.

Sean stood at the lounge doorway and had another drink, while Greg stood at the front door, now slightly ajar. Sean was making him wait, waiting for him to crack even the tiniest bit. But Greg kept everything in. He sucked the anxiety and everything else down inside him like a vacuum, not daring to let it out.

They stared at each other up and down the hallway.

Sean stared at him, leaning up against the doorframe.

For a moment, neither said a word.

It seemed like an eternity for Greg, wondering if he would crack and let Sean into what he was really feeling.

Sean then said; 'Tell the bitch she can have the bloody divorce then. Who gives a fuckin' shit?'

Greg suddenly felt an incredible rush, but he didn't think it was of excitement, it was like an enormous crash, all the anxieties falling through the pit of his stomach, like an avalanche, and his heart practically leapt out of his mouth. But almost at the same time, he had a terrible feeling that Sean had seen it, that his rush, that everything that had happened inside him had caused him to crack, but somehow, he remained calm, and managed to sustain his bland expression. Which was far from easy. He couldn't afford excitement yet.

'You two idiots deserve each other. Get out of my sight, both of you. We'll see if you last. She wasn't even much good at sex. Why'd'ya think I had to get my own satisfaction half the time? You wait, you'll be doing the same thing before long,' Sean dared him, very self-satisfied.

'I don't hit women,' Greg said, deciding not to rise to the remark, and he was about to go, but quickly added, 'It's really the next woman you hurt I feel sorry for. My only concern was for Carol. I love her. But the next one probably won't be so fortunate. You will meet someone else, men like you always do, I don't understand why. But I'm just glad I was able to meet Carol before it was too late. She'll file for divorce tomorrow morning.' His tone was grim. Sean just sneered. And without saying another word, he then left.

Greg was all smiles as he walked back to his car. But the smiles were purely of relief. It may not be all over yet of course, as there was going to be a long wait yet before the divorce could be final, but at least a long, hard and bitter one could hopefully now be avoided.

He puffed out his relief and sighed heavily. He couldn't wait to tell Carol the marvellous news. She would be so relieved.

When Carol heard the front door go, she closed her eyes, almost trying to will Greg to bring good news, and slowly got up from the sofa, where she had sat worrying herself half to death right from the time he had gone.

She walked into the hallway and saw Greg standing there, hands in his pockets, head down and wiping his feet on the doormat. He looked up at her.

'Hi there,' he said.

She grinned thinly.

'What did he say?' she asked, quietly, anxiously, not liking the look of this.

'Well, actually, I did most of the talking.'

Carol just looked at him, anxiously.

Greg then raised the corners of his mouth into a grin.

'I don't believe it,' she said, in hardly a whisper. 'He said yes?'

'After a bit of persuasion, yes,' Greg said with a grin.

Carol suddenly felt her eyes swim out of focus. A strange dizziness overcame her as the relief flooded through her mind, then her body, instantly causing another bizarre floating sensation, but without the added anxiety and tension of last night.

Carol still couldn't believe it. All the pain, the fear, and all the tension stored inside her for so long, suddenly disappeared in a matter of seconds, made her feel as if this moment wasn't real at all, but part of a dream. Thankfully it was real. She knew that in reality the divorce would take time and that being married again may still have its ups and downs, but she didn't care. There was a feeling that it would be eternal happiness being with Greg, day in, day out. Carol couldn't help but get carried away with it. The relief of it all, the tremendous sudden release from such a heavy burden. She almost couldn't breathe. Just the thought of it made her feel light-headed. Although, she felt like losing control. And why shouldn't she? There was no reason not to, but there was every reason to do so.

'Oh, *Greg*!' Carol shrieked, the relief almost forcing the words out. She wanted to run up to Greg, and throw her arms around his neck, but she couldn't. She wasn't going to move. She almost wanted to collapse right there, and allow her mind to float back up.

She put her hands to her face and wept. She could sense Greg coming towards her, which was fine, because, amazingly, she couldn't go to him. He held her and that's when she threw her arms around him and held on. Held. Held.

She was well aware of the reality of this. Waiting forever for the divorce to settle. Arranging everything afterwards. But a new journey awaited, and soon, the journey would begin, and Carol knew that she could make it work. After last night, she knew. If she couldn't be certain about anything else, she could be certain about that. She held him tight, holding onto that thought.

Right now, a strange, but intriguing and possibly exciting future now lay ahead. And of course, he would have her. For a brief moment, that made her shiver with a thrilling, sexy nervousness.

Married life with Greg was going to be full of interesting possibilities.

www.ingramcontent.com/pod-product-compliance
Ingram Content Group UK Ltd.
Pitfield, Milton Keynes, MK11 3LW, UK
UKHW020225250726
13967UKWH00001B/188

9 781785 078439